GREAT STORIES for kids

Book Five

JERRY D. THOMAS

Pacific Press Publishing Association
Boise, Idaho
Oshawa, Ontario, Canada

Editor: Aileen Andres Sox
Designer: Robert N. Mason
Illustration/Art Direction: Justinen Creative Group
Typeset in Century Old Style 13/17

ISBN 0-8163-1209-5

97 98 99 00 01 • 5 4 3 2

Dedication

To all the little people who inspired these stories:

First, to my own wonderful children—Jonathan, Jennifer, and Jeremy—who aren't so little anymore. Not all the stories are about them—just the good ones.

And then to my brothers and sisters—in memory of the days when we were kids and of the escapades we shared. Also, to my nieces and nephews on both sides of the family— thanks for the stories you inspired.

Finally, to all the kids who will read these stories or hear them read. May the stories bring you smiles, laughter, help in difficult situations, hope for a bright tomorrow, and a belief in the never-ending love of God.

A few words of thanks:

To the management of Pacific Press for having the vision to publish this set.

To Aileen Andres Sox, who encouraged me from the beginning.

To Robert Mason for a design that will drag kids right into the pages.

To Lars and Kim Justinen and their creative group for the outstanding art that brings the stories to life.

And most of all, to my wife, Kitty, for her love and patient endurance while these stories were being written.

Contents

Tornado Warning

I t's a long fly ball to center field," Sean shouted to himself as he threw his baseball as high as he could. He drifted backward to catch it. "The center fielder goes back . . ."

Then his foot hit the border around the flower bed. Sean went over backward right into the flowers. "Ooof." The ball hit the roof of the house.

"Hey, did you see it?" Sean called to his sister, Bethany.

"Did I see you trip over your own feet and lose the game?" Bethany called from where she was sitting on the tree swing. "Yes, I did."

"No." Sean sat up and brushed off the dirt. "Did you see where my ball went?"

"Yep. It went right into the gutter of the roof." Bethany swung back and forth. "And you'll never get it down."

"Yes, I will," Sean started to say. But a flash of light stopped their argument. *Boom!* "Wow, where did that thunderstorm come from? It wasn't there a few minutes ago." Bethany

Dealing with emergencies

walked over to where he was standing and looked up.

"Those clouds are really moving fast. Sean, have you ever seen the sky look green like that?"

Sean shook his head. "That is weird." The sky seemed to get darker every second. When a lightning bolt ripped across the dark green clouds and the thunder crashed around them, they both made the same decision.

"I'm going inside!"

But even inside, they both stared out the front windows. "This is scary," Bethany said. "And Mom's not home from the store yet."

"Maybe we should listen for a weather report on TV," Sean said. With a push of a remote-control button, the TV snapped on.

The newsperson was speaking. "This just in. At least two tornadoes have been spotted in our area. Everyone should seek shelter immediately."

Sean and Bethany stared at each other. "Where do we go?" Bethany whispered. The man on the TV kept talking.

"If you are outdoors, get inside if you can. If not, lie down in the nearest ditch and cover your head. If you are inside, move away from all windows and glass. Take shelter in the basement if you have one or in a bathroom, hallway, or closet that is small and well-protected. I repeat . . ." Suddenly, the TV and all the lights went out.

Bethany screamed and ran toward Sean. The darkness got deeper, and the wind began to howl. "What do we do?" Bethany shouted.

"What did the guy on the TV say?" Sean tried to think. "He said we could hide in a bathroom or closet, right? Come on!"

As they ran past her bedroom, Bethany stopped. "Wait! Remember when Grandma talked about the tornado that almost hit her house? She said they got in the bathtub and pulled a mattress over their heads."

"That's right! Let's grab your mattress." As they wrestled it off the bed, the wind stopped blowing, and everything was very still.

"Is the storm gone?" Bethany whispered. Sean turned and looked out the window.

"It's still dark," he said, "and the clouds are still—" Then he saw it, and his tongue stopped working. A long, dark funnel reached down from the clouds like an elephant's trunk. As he stared, the tornado moved closer. It was coming straight toward them.

"Sean, what is it?" Bethany leaned past him to see. Her scream snapped Sean out of it.

"Tornado! Come on! Grab the mattress!" They drug it out

the bedroom door and started down the hall.

Then they heard a loud noise, like a train was coming right through their house. "Drop it," Sean shouted. He shoved Bethany to the floor and pulled the mattress over them.

"We need to pray, Sean," Bethany said. She closed her eyes and whispered, "Please God, keep us safe. Keep Mom safe. Keep everyone safe in this storm, Amen."

"Amen," Sean repeated.

For a long minute, the house shook and banged and crashed. Then the roaring wind died away, and everything was quieter again. Sean was so scared he thought he was going to faint. "Are you OK?" he whispered. Bethany nodded. Her face was so white it almost glowed. "Let's get out of here, then."

They pushed back the mattress slowly, almost afraid of what was out there. "Everything looks OK," Sean said as he stood up. "Maybe the tornado missed us."

Bethany followed a strange glow coming from the living room. "What is . . . oh, wow!"

The living room was filled with green leaves. Leaves still attached to branches. A whole tree had crashed through the roof. Right in front of the television hung Bethany's swing, swaying back and forth.

Bethany blinked three times. "So, want to swing?" She giggled nervously.

Then there was another roaring sound from outside. They both jumped and stared out the open front door. "It's not coming back, is it?" Bethany asked.

But this roaring was smaller, and it was coming down the street. Suddenly, their mom's van raced up the sidewalk and right across the yard. "Mom!" they both shouted as they ran out into the rain.

"Sean! Bethany!" She jumped out and threw her arms around them. "I was so scared for you," she cried. "I was praying the whole way home. Are you OK?" When she decided they were, she looked at the house. "Is that the swing tree?" she asked.

"Yes," Bethany answered. "But don't worry. The swing's OK. It's in the living room."

Sean looked up at the sky. In spite of the rain, it was getting lighter. The storm seemed to be passing. "What are we going to do about the house?" he asked.

His mother stared at it for a second, then shook her head. "We're not going to worry about it. You're both safe, and that's all that matters. Insurance will take care of whatever's broken. Come on. We'll go to Grandma's. Then I'll call for help to get our stuff out of the rain."

As Sean walked around to the other side of the van, he almost tripped over something. "Hey, it's my baseball!" He held it up to show Bethany. "See, I told you I'd get it back."

Bethany rolled her eyes. "But you had to use my tree to do it."

Tornado Safety Rules

1. If you are outdoors, get inside if you can. If not, lie down in the nearest ditch and cover your head.
2. Never try to outrun a tornado in a car. Get out and seek shelter.
3. If you are inside, move away from all windows and glass. Take shelter in the basement if you have one or in a bathroom, hallway, or closet that is small and well protected.

WET EXPLOSION

F irecracker snorted and shook his big brown head. Water sprayed in all directions. "Hey!" Stefanie yelled at the horse. "Cut that out. You're the one who wanted a drink, not me."

Wheehick! Firecracker gave his own special laugh.

Stefanie grabbed the horse's lead rope and led him away from the pond. "Mrs. Bailey was right. You are tricky." She shook the water off her arm and pulled a red apple out of her back pocket. Taking one big bite, she chewed slowly and offered the rest to Firecracker. He wrapped his long teeth around it and crunched it down. Mrs. Bailey had said Firecracker could have one

Learning patience

apple each day.

Ever since Stefanie's family moved into their house, she had watched the beautiful brown horse in the pasture just outside her window. His fence came so close to their house she could talk to Firecracker without getting out of bed.

Even though Stefanie shared an apple with the horse every day, for years she could only dream of riding him. Firecracker belonged to their neighbors, the Baileys. This summer, their son had gone to college, leaving no one to take care of the horse. Stefanie had volunteered (begged) for the job.

"I don't know," her mom had said. "You won't be able to just jump up on Firecracker the first day and ride. You would have to be patient and work hard." She gave Stefanie one of those "remember-what-happened-last-time" looks.

Stefanie didn't know if her mom was thinking about last year's piano lessons or her tomato-plant project. She didn't ask.

"That's true," Mrs. Bailey had agreed. "Firecracker is a gentle horse, but he's tricky, especially since he hasn't been ridden much lately. He likes people, but he's naughty with inexperienced riders. You'd have to take time to learn how to ride him and make him behave."

"Oh, I'd be very patient," Stefanie had insisted. "I'll take as much time as Firecracker needs." *Right up until the day before the parade*, she had added to herself.

"We need each other," she said to the horse as he chewed. "You need someone to take care of you, and I need a ride in the Independence Day parade."

Firecracker wisely said nothing.

"Hey, Stef," a voice called from behind them, "is that your horse?"

Stefanie recognized Nathan's voice and turned. "Hi. No,

Firecracker belongs to the Baileys, but I'm taking care of him."

"Firecracker?" Nathan teased. "He looks more like a dud."

Stefanie put her hands on her hips. "We'll see who looks like a dud in the Independence Day parade. You'll be riding in your wagon behind that goat again, won't you?"

"At least I'll be in the parade," Nathan replied. "You'll be on the sidewalk, as usual."

"I'll be riding Firecracker," Stefanie said haughtily.

Nathan snorted. "Yeah, right. You probably don't even know how to ride a horse."

"I do too!"

"Prove it," Nathan challenged.

By this time, Stefanie had learned how to saddle Firecracker. She whirled around and marched into the shed to get his saddle. The horse didn't object to the saddle blanket being spread across his back. He didn't flinch when the saddle was placed on top and cinched up. Firecracker never moved a muscle.

"That's a good boy," Stefanie said quietly. "I have to ride you now to prove that Nathan's wrong. You'll help me, won't you? Remember all those nice apples I gave you? Steady, now."

"What are you waiting for?" Nathan called from the fence. "I think you're afraid to even get on the horse."

Stefanie reached for the saddle horn and put her foot in the stirrup. "I hope you brought some ketchup. You'll need to eat those words." With a big jump, she threw her leg over and pulled herself up onto the saddle. Quickly, she grabbed the reins and tensed for whatever Firecracker would do.

Firecracker did nothing.

"Come on, boy," Stefanie said softly. She clicked the reins.

"Let's go."

Firecracker just stood there.

"Maybe you should push the gas pedal." Nathan hooted.

Stefanie kicked lightly with her heels. "Come on," she pleaded. Finally, she threw her hands up in the air.

As soon as she let go of the reins, Firecracker exploded. He took off as fast as he could go, heading straight back across the pasture toward the pond. Stefanie grabbed the saddle horn and barely managed to hang on.

"Whoa! Slow down, slow down!"

Firecracker ran even faster.

Stefanie saw the pond getting closer and closer. Firecracker wasn't turning one way or the other. "Whoa! Stop!" she shouted.

Just before his feet hit the water, Firecracker stopped.

Stefanie didn't.

One second, she was holding onto the saddle horn. The next second, she was flying over Firecracker's head.

2-G.S.K. ENGv5

Splat! Water and mud exploded in all directions. Birds scattered, frogs jumped, fish dove. For a moment, Stefanie disappeared in the spray. What was left after the splash didn't look like Stefanie at all. Water dripped off the lilies that were stuck in her hair. She wiped the mud off her face and opened her eyes.

Wheehick! Firecracker stood on the shore, almost smiling.

"Ha-hah-hah!" Nathan was rolling on the grass, laughing like a hyena. "And you think I'll look funny with a goat?" he shouted. "If you can ride that horse in the parade, I'll eat my hat!"

Stefanie just turned and sloshed toward her own house, leaving them both behind. When she got to the kitchen door, she pushed it open and stood dripping on the porch.

"Stefanie!" Her mother almost dropped the phone. "Are you OK?" She said goodbye and hung up. After a few seconds to be sure that Stefanie wasn't injured, she asked, "What happened?"

Stefanie pointed toward the pond.

"You tried to ride Firecracker," her mother guessed.

Stefanie stared at her own mud-covered shoes. "I'm through with that horse! He's just too dumb or too stubborn. I'm not ever going back over there."

HAT EATER

A re you sure you aren't hurt?" Stefanie's mother asked again.

Other than being soaking wet and covered with mud, Stefanie was fine. She nodded, already thinking about a nice hot shower. So her mother's next words were shocking.

"Then you are marching yourself right back over there. You can't leave that horse standing out in the field. You promised Mrs. Bailey that you would take care of Firecracker. After you put the saddle away and make sure the horse is taken care of, you can go tell Mrs. Bailey that you changed your mind. But I'll be very disappointed if you do."

Stefanie opened her mouth, but the look on her mother's face kept the words inside. She turned and sloshed back across the field.

Nathan was gone, and Stefanie went through the motions without speaking to Firecracker. When he nuzzled her arm,

Learning patience

Hat Eater

she ignored him.

Mom knew I would do this, Stefanie thought, *because I've always done it before. Patience and hard work. Why can't I be patient enough to do the things I really want to do?*

When she was done, she rang Mrs. Bailey's doorbell. Mrs. Bailey took one look at her and said, "You tried to ride him, right?"

Stefanie nodded. "I can't do it. I wanted to ride him in the Independence Day parade, but he won't listen to me."

Mrs. Bailey tilted her head and thought. "My son had ways of making Firecracker behave. We still have several weeks before the parade. I could show you some things, but it would take . . ."

"I know, I know," Stefanie interrupted. "Patience and hard work. Would you show me? I promise to do just as you say. No matter how long it takes."

"Even if you still aren't ready to ride in the parade?" Mrs. Bailey asked.

Stefanie took a deep breath. "Yes. I'm going to stick with it this time."

"Great! What we need first is something to reward Firecracker with when he does the right things. Can you think of something he likes?"

Stefanie smiled.

In the weeks that followed, Stefanie's time was spent leading Firecracker around the pasture, first without the saddle, then with it.

"Let's try tying a heavy bag of grain on the saddle," Mrs. Bailey said. "Maybe for Firecracker, it will feel like someone sitting on his back."

The horse stood still until the bag was in place. Then he raced and stopped like he had with Stefanie. The bag held on, so Firecracker tried it again. Finally, he stopped and refused to move until the bag was off.

They tried another plan. Stefanie spent some time sitting in the saddle on Firecracker's back while he was tied to a post. Then Mrs. Bailey took the reins and led the horse around the pasture. After a few days of that, Mrs. Bailey handed the reins to Stefanie.

"See what he'll do."

They found out quickly enough. Firecracker did nothing. As long as Stefanie held the reins, he stood still. "I'm not turning loose of the reins," Stefanie said with a glance at the pond. "Not after what happened last time."

The next morning, one of Stefanie's friends called during breakfast. "Can you go to the swimming pool with us today?"

Stefanie only had to think about the cool water for a second before she opened her mouth to say Yes. But before she said a word, the sound of Firecracker's whinny came in through the window.

"I can't," Stefanie said to her friend. "I'm working on a special project for the parade." With a big sigh, she hung up the phone. *Is this really worth it?* she asked herself as she

trudged over to Firecracker's shed.

By the time Stefanie finished brushing Firecracker, Mrs. Bailey was getting the saddle out of the shed. "You're not ready to give up, are you, Stefanie?" she asked.

Stefanie shrugged and tried to smile. "It doesn't seem like anything will teach Firecracker to let me ride. At least, not in time for the parade."

"I have one more idea," Mrs. Bailey said. "This one just might work. Come on. I'll explain the plan."

When it finally arrived, Independence Day brought perfect weather for a parade. Stefanie bumped into Nathan as the parade floats and bands were lining up. "Hey, how do you like my suit?" Nathan asked.

Stefanie laughed at his long floppy shoes and bright yellow hat. "You look like a clown. Is your goat dressed up too?"

Nathan grinned. "Of course. Hey, where's that horse you were going to ride? Still down at the pond?"

"You'll see," was all Stefanie would say.

When the parade started, Stefanie mounted Firecracker and waited in line with the other horses. "Now behave yourself," she whispered in his ear. When the signal came to move, the other horses stepped forward. Firecracker stood still.

Stefanie reached behind her and got the stick she had tied to her saddle. Tied to the stick was a shiny red apple. "OK, Firecracker, let's go." She held the stick out and dangled the apple in front of the horse's nose.

Firecracker stretched his neck and took a step toward the apple. When it moved, he took another step and another. Soon they were in step behind the others.

Stefanie waved to her mother and Mrs. Bailey in the crowd on Main Street.

"I'm so proud of you," her mother shouted.

"Don't drop the apple," Mrs. Bailey called.

Stefanie smiled and waved until her face hurt and her arm ached. But she was too happy to stop.

"Hey, you did ride in the parade," Nathan called out as they reached the end. He patted Firecracker's neck. "I didn't think you would ever get this horse to obey."

Stefanie stroked the horse's mane. "I wasn't sure I could either at first. It just took a lot of patience and hard work." The way she sounded surprised even her. "And it was worth it."

"Well," Nathan said, "you both looked great. I guess I will have to eat my hat. Hey!"

While Nathan was talking, the horse had reached back and snatched off his big yellow hat. When Firecracker chewed, Stefanie laughed. "I guess Firecracker beat you to it."

Wheehick! Firecracker laughed too.

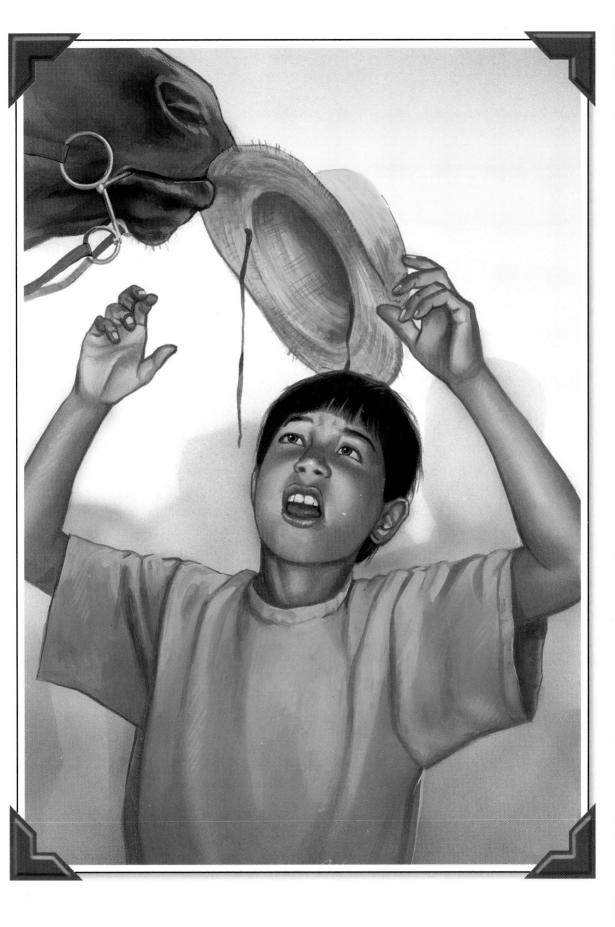

Beautiful and Mysterious

Did you get them?"

Sonia's voice hissed like a leaking bicycle tire. She raced down the alleyway after Alyssa.

Alyssa finally stopped behind a big dumpster. "Here," she said, pulling two slightly mangled cigarettes out of her pocket. "I don't think anyone saw me."

Sonia took one and smoothed it out straight. "How do I look?" she asked, putting the cigarette between her lips. "Do I look beautiful and mysterious, like the woman in that magazine?"

"No," Alyssa answered. "The magazine woman is holding her cigarette like this." She raised her arm and dangled her cigarette between two fingers. "It's very glamorous."

Slam!

Both girls jumped like they had been shot. Sonia grabbed Alyssa's arm. "What was that?" she whispered.

"It sounded like the back door of my house," Alyssa said.

Dealing with smoking

"Come on. Let's go."

Sonia held out her cigarette. "Here, you keep this."

"No way," Alyssa said. She threw both cigarettes into the dumpster and led the way back toward her house. "Look, my Uncle Tim's on the back porch smoking."

Sonia clutched Alyssa's arm. "You don't think he knows you took those cigarettes, do you?"

"Ow! Stop strangling my arm. No, I took them out of an old pack he threw in the trash. Come on. Let's go talk to him."

The girls walked up to the porch. "Good evening, girls," Tim said. "What are you up to this time?"

Sonia gasped. Alyssa punched her arm and said, "Not much. Just wandering around the neighborhood." She watched him flick ashes onto the grass.

Tim nodded. "I'm just out catching a smoke, myself. You know your mother won't let me smoke in the house."

"Why do you smoke, Uncle Tim?" Alyssa asked. She watched his face carefully.

He took another puff. "I guess it relaxes me, kind of calms me down." He chuckled and pulled the pack out of his shirt pocket. "It's funny to be calmed by something that says it could kill you right on the package."

Alyssa had read the warning about lung cancer and emphysema.

Uncle Tim laughed again. "But you never think it'll happen to you. And so far, so good." He tossed the butt into a trash can and headed back in. "I'd better be headed home. See you girls later."

"I have to go in too," Alyssa said to Sonia. "I'll see you tomorrow."

In her room, Alyssa opened the magazine with the picture and laid it on her bed. The woman's beautiful face, perfect smile, and elegant fingernails shone out from the page. Between her fingers was a long white cigarette. The words said *She's beautiful and mysterious—the Elegance Cigarette woman.*

Alyssa picked up a pencil and held it between her fingers. "Why, yes, I'd love to," she said in a deep, soft voice.

"You'd love to what?" The voice crashed in on Alyssa's imagination. She dropped the pencil and fell back onto the bed.

"Mom! You scared me to death!"

"Sorry," her mother said. "Who were you talking to, anyway?"

Alyssa leaned across the open magazine. "I was talking to myself."

Her mother's eyebrows went up. "I see. Well, supper's ready. Come and eat."

After supper, Alyssa read another magazine while her dad watched TV. She looked up when a commercial showed a beautiful woman with a perfect smile. "New Perfect-White tooth cleaner will make your smile shine. Just apply for thirty minutes once a month."

"That sounded easier than brushing your teeth every day," she said out loud.

Her mother snorted. "As long as you want perfect white teeth with holes in them."

The woman on the commercial added, "It even works on smokers' teeth!"

"Do smokers have dirty teeth?" Alyssa asked.

"Have you ever looked at your Uncle Tim's teeth?" Dad asked. "They're as yellow as a beaver's. That's what the smoke does to them if you smoke long enough."

"And to your fingers too," her mom added. She held up

Beautiful and Mysterious

two fingers. "Most smokers have yellow stains on the fingers they hold their cigarettes with."

"Ugh," Alyssa said. *There must be a way to keep that from happening,* she thought. *After all, that model in the magazine has beautiful teeth and fingers.*

The next morning, Sonia called. "Alyssa, it's too hot to just sit around the house. Let's go to the pool."

"Wait a second. I'll ask my mom." She put her hand over the phone. "Mom! Can I go to the pool with Sonia?"

"I don't have time to take you," Mom called back.

Alyssa thought for a second. "I could take the bus. It goes right to the city park."

"OK," Mom answered. "But you have to be back by three."

Before long, Alyssa was sitting on a city bus next to someone's grandmother. She pulled the magazine out of her backpack and turned to the model with the cigarette. *I could be beautiful and mysterious,* she said to herself.

Holding two fingers up to her lips, Alyssa pretended to puff on a cigarette.

"She looks glamorous, doesn't she?" a voice croaked in her ear.

"Ah!" Alyssa jerked away. It was the grandmother. "I'm sorry. You scared me."

"I do sound strange, don't I?" the woman said. "I saw you looking at the model. I used to be a model." She croaked a laugh at the look on Alyssa's face. "It was a long time ago. But I used to model clothes. And cigarettes, like that woman."

"What happened to your voice?" Alyssa asked.

The woman pulled back a scarf to show a shiny metal circle on her throat. "I have to breathe through this thing," she explained. "When I got throat cancer, the doctors had to take out my voice box."

Alyssa's hand went up to her own throat.

"You see," the woman went on, "I didn't just model for cigarette companies. I smoked the cigarettes too. And this is what happened. It's really glamorous, don't you think?"

Alyssa found Sonia in the pool changing room. "Look," Sonia said. She reached into her pack. "I found a cigarette in the laundromat." She held one up to her lips. "Do I look mysterious and alluring?"

Alyssa slapped it out of her hand. "You look stupid. Don't ever smoke one of those!"

Sonia's eyes got really big.

Alyssa laughed. "Let me explain."

Water Balloon Battle

Bombs away!"

Luke ducked, but the water balloon landed right on the back of his neck. *Splat!* "Now you've done it, Holly!" Luke shouted up at the tree where his sister sat laughing. "It's time for a full-scale attack."

Holly dropped to the ground and ran for the corner of the house. She dodged two blue balloons and was almost there when a big red one hit her right in the middle of the back. *Sploosh!*

"Yes!" Luke

Being courteous

shouted. "Now we're even."

"Now, we're out of balloons," Holly said, walking slowly back toward him. Her left arm reached behind her toward the wet spot. "The water really feels good on a hot day, don't you think?"

"Yeah, you're right," Luke agreed.

"Then you'll enjoy this!" Holly whipped a little blue balloon

from behind her back and popped it right on Luke's head.

Splop! Water dripped into Luke's eyes. "Holly!" Then he smiled. "Thanks for cooling me off."

"Luke! Holly!" their mother called from the front door, "come in and eat lunch."

"Aw, Mom," Luke moaned, "the water balloon war was just

getting started."

"Come on," she called again. "The sun won't disappear before you finish a sandwich."

In the house, they raced to the table. "Whoosh!" Luke said. "It's really warm out there—almost like last summer. Will you get me a drink, Mom?"

Mom stared at him. "If that's how you ask, you can pour your own juice. You'll find it in the refrigerator."

"Yeah, you rude boy," Holly said. "Mother, may I have some juice, please?"

"Luke can get it for you, since he's getting some anyway."

Luke stuck his tongue out at Holly and got the juice. Then he poured himself and Holly each a glassful. "Took you long enough," Holly said.

Luke just glared at her and drank his whole glassful without stopping. "Aaaah, that was good." Then he burped.

Mom threw down her towel. "That does it. The two of you have completely forgotten what it means to be polite." She held up her hand when they both started making excuses. "I don't want to hear it. For the rest of this day, every time either of you open your mouth, I want to hear the words *please* or *thank you*."

Luke opened his mouth, then closed it. Holly raised her hand. "Mother, may I please eat my lunch?" She nodded, and they both started eating.

"I'd like to go back out as soon as I get finished eating, please," Luke said. "We're having a water balloon war, and I'm winning."

"No, you're not!" Holly said. Then she remembered. "I'll thank you to remember who's the wettest."

Mom said, "I hope you're not forgetting our deal, guys."

"We're not, thank you," Holly said. They were saving money to buy sleds before winter. Mom had promised to pay them to rake up the leaves in the yard, but only if they did it every weekend of the fall. "We'll rake first, then play."

After lunch, Mom met them in the garage with a handful of big garbage bags. "It'll be easier if you rake the leaves into small piles and pick them up instead of making one big pile. Then you won't be tempted to stop working and jump in it."

Luke and Holly exchanged an embarrassed look. Last week, they had raked the leaves into a big pile that everyone wanted to jump into. When the fun was over, they had to rake the whole yard over again.

"Thank you for reminding us," Luke said. He pulled the rakes out from behind some boxes and handed one to his sister. "Let's get started, please."

Holly started raking by the porch. "You start by the sidewalk, please," she said to Luke. After ten minutes of work, Luke brought a trash bag over to pick up her leaves.

"Psst," he whispered. "Are we really going to do this 'please' and 'thank you' thing all day?"

"I am," Holly whispered back. "But I'm going to make you forget and get in trouble. I'm going to win this war too."

"No way. But thanks for the idea," Luke said. Then he threw a whole armful of leaves in her face.

"Aahh!" Holly jumped back and pulled the leaves out of her hair. "Please don't do that again. Or I'll do this!" She grabbed the half-full trash bag by the bottom and swung it at him. Leaves went everywhere.

By the time they stopped, the yard was covered with leaves and the bag was empty. "Ugh," Holly said, "thanks to you, we have to start over."

"Me? You were the one who emptied the bag. Thank you very much." Luke went back to his rake, and for a few minutes, leaves actually got raked and bagged.

"You guys are almost finished." Mom stepped out carrying a pitcher clinking with ice cubes in one hand and cups in the other. "Very good. Would you like some ice water?"

"Yes, please," Luke answered. They each filled a cup and emptied it.

"Thank you very much, Mother," Holly said.

Mom looked around the yard and across the street. "I have an idea. Mr. Andross's yard hasn't been raked at all yet. Why don't you two go and rake it for him?"

Luke looked across the street at Mr. Andross's house. He couldn't remember seeing him outside in a long time. "Do you think he would pay us?" he asked. Then he added, "Thank you for the idea."

Mom smiled. "Very good, Luke. I don't know. But I think it would be a good thing to do even if you don't get paid."

Holly was looking too. "It's not a very big yard. It would only take a few minutes. If you would let us, please."

Luke agreed. "Thanks or no thanks, let's do it."

Mom went to Mr. Andross's door to tell him what was going on. When Luke bent down to pick up his rake, a handful of ice cubes went down the back of his shirt.

He jumped straight up. "Holly! I'm going to . . ."

Mom turned to see what the shouting was about. Luke was stuck with his mouth open and his back freezing.

Water Balloon Battle

Ambushed!

Luke hopped on one foot and finished his sentence. "I'm going to be a lot cooler now, thank you very much." Holly was laughing too hard to say anything at all. Mom just smiled and went back to the house.

They had most of the leaves bagged up when Luke saw Mr. Andross waving at them from a window. He waved back. Mr. Andross opened the window just enough to shout, "Be sure to get the leaves under those bushes." Then he closed the window and disappeared.

"You're welcome," Luke muttered as he raked under the bushes. "All this hard work, for free probably, and he didn't even

Being courteous

say 'thank you.'"

Holly agreed. "He doesn't sound like a real nice person. Let's hurry up and get finished, please."

While Luke went to get more bags, Holly threw one of the full bags over her shoulder and carried it to the edge of the sidewalk. Then the window opened again. "Hey, girl, don't put that bag there. My trash bags have to be on the other side of the driveway."

"You could at least say please," Holly mumbled as she picked it up again. She kept carrying bags while Luke filled up one more with the last of Mr. Andross's leaves.

"Please tell me that's the last bag," she said as Luke tied it closed.

"This is it, thanks to me," Luke said.

Holly had only taken a few steps when she felt something wet running down her leg. "What in the world?" she started to say. Then she dropped the bag. Water spurted out through a hole in the bottom. "Luke! You got my pants all wet! Stop it, please."

He just laughed. "You can thank me for emptying the pitcher of water into the bag before I put the leaves in. And poking a hole in it. I knew it would please you."

When everything was put away, there was a race for empty balloons and the garden hose. Luke ducked behind a tree. "Thanks, you missed me," he called when a balloon sailed over his head. The next one hit him in the face. "Thanks for nothing," he mumbled.

Holly hid behind the car. A balloon sailed past. "Oh, please, that wasn't even close," she called. Then Luke rolled one under the car, and it broke on her shoe. "Yuck," she said. "Please don't do that again."

The battle went on, filled with shouts of "please" and "thank you," until it was time to come in and clean up for supper.

"Mom," Luke called from his room, "could you tell me where my green shirt is? Please?"

She tossed him the shirt with a smile. Holly called from her room, "Mom, are my new blue jeans in the wash? Please help me find them." In just a minute, they appeared in Holly's room.

"Supper's on the table," Dad called from the kitchen. "Come and get it."

"Thanks for making supper," Luke said as he dug into his

spaghetti. "I'm starving."

"So am I," Holly said, "so stop hogging the butter, Luke. And pass it to me, please."

Dad looked surprised. "Aren't we a polite family tonight?"

"Yes, we are," Mom answered with a smile. "And not only did these two rake our yard today, they also raked Mr. Andross's."

"But we're not doing it again," Luke announced. "He just demanded that we do a good job. He didn't even say 'thank you.' "

"He didn't ask us to do things," Holly added. "He just told us to. He didn't even say 'please.' "

Mom raised one eyebrow. "You mean it matters to you whether or not someone says 'please' when they ask you to do something?"

Luke nodded with his mouth full of bread. He swallowed before he spoke. "If they don't say 'please,' they're just ordering you around like a slave."

Mom nodded. "And when you do something for someone and they don't even bother to thank you, it makes you mad?"

"That's right," Holly agreed. "It makes me decide not to do things for them anymore, thank you very much."

"Hmmm." Dad took a drink. "Well, that makes you want to be sure that you always thank the people who help you, doesn't it?"

Holly nodded. Luke nodded. Mom nodded. "Since we all agree, I have something to tell you. When I talked to Mr. Andross, he wanted me to thank you both for raking his leaves. And he promised to pay you every week if you keep raking them."

"Great!" Luke said. "Now we'll get those sleds for sure. Thanks, Mom."

"That even sounded like you meant it, Luke. See how nice it is to live in a house where people are polite? Now, Holly, it's your turn to wash and Luke's turn to rinse. Please do a good job, both of you."

Holly piled the dishes into the soapy water. "Please don't think you're the winner yet," she hissed. "The war's not over yet."

"Thanks for telling me," Luke whispered back. Then he aimed the sprayer at her and pulled the trigger.

"Aaah!" When she blinked the water off her eyelashes, Holly tossed a cup of soapy water right on Luke's shirt.

The water flew back and forth until there was more on the counter and floor than in the sink. Suddenly, their mother's voice came in through the window.

"Luke! Holly! Come out here this minute."

"Now you've done it," Holly said. "Thanks to you, we're both in trouble."

As they stepped off the porch, Mom stepped out from behind a tree. *Splat! Splot!* Water balloons hit them both right in the chest.

"Mom!" they both shouted.

"I win!" Mom said. Then she laughed, "and you have to mop the kitchen."

Luke and Holly just stared at each other. They could only think of one thing to say. "Thanks a lot!"

Breathe In, Breathe Out

Come on, Merrie!" Angelina called. "Sink this one!"

Merrie dribbled the ball once, then once again. She tried to concentrate, but she was breathing too fast. *Breathe in—hweeh*, she told herself, *breathe out—hwooh. Hweeh-hwooh.* She launched the ball toward the hoop. It clanged off the front side.

"Grab it!" Angelina shouted. But someone from the other team snatched it before Merrie could. She turned and raced down the court after her teammates.

Hweeh-hwooh-hweeh-hwooh. Merrie arrived under the basket just as the shot went up. The ball hit the backboard and rolled off the rim. Leaping up with both hands high, Merrie grabbed it. Without hesitating, she dribbled off to her right and headed toward the goal.

Hweeh-hweeh-hweeh-hwooh. "Merrie! Pass!" Angelina shouted. Merrie launched the ball to her teammate waiting under the basket. *Swish!* An easy basket!

**Dealing with life and unfairness;
dealing with handicaps in self or others**

"Nice pass, Merrie," Angelina said as she ran by. "Hey, are you OK? You look kind of funny."

"I'm-*hweeh-hweeh*-fine," Merrie said. "Let's go!" But by the time she had run up and down the court another time, Merrie wasn't fine. *Hweeh-hweeh-hweeh-hweeh!* She was breathing too fast, but she wasn't getting enough air. The gymnasium started to spin. Merrie knelt down so she wouldn't fall over.

"Merrie!" Angelina ran to her. "Are you OK?"

Hweeh-hweeh-hweeh-hweeh! Merrie couldn't answer. She couldn't get in enough air to speak.

"Time out!" Angelina shouted. "Coach! Coach Swain! Come here quick—something's wrong with Merrie!"

It didn't take long for Coach Swain to figure out that Merrie was having trouble breathing. She pointed to Angelina. "Go call the school nurse. Tell her it's an emergency!"

Merrie tried to talk. "I'll-*hweeh*-be-*hweeh*-OK."

"Why don't you try to lie down here," Coach Swain said. "All right, everyone back off. Give her some air." She helped Merrie lie back on the floor and knelt down beside her. "The nurse will be here in minute—there she is now."

Mrs. Lorentz didn't waste any time. "Merrie, how are you feeling?" she asked as she hooked a blood-pressure cuff to Merrie's arm. "Is it your asthma?"

Merrie nodded.

"You were playing basketball, right? And you didn't stop when you should have?"

Merrie nodded again.

"Where's your medicine? Your inhaler?" The look on Merrie's face said it all. "You left them at home." Mrs. Lorentz took the cuff off. "You've got your heart racing mighty fast, Merrie. And I don't have to tell you how much trouble you're having breathing. I think you should go down to the emergency room so they can help you get your breathing back to normal."

Merrie shook her head. "I'll-*hweeh*-be-*hweeh*-OK."

"I'm sorry, Merrie, but we can't take any chances. I'll call your mother's office and tell her to meet you there."

If Merrie's face hadn't already been red from trying to breathe, it would have turned red now. *How embarrassing,* she thought. *I don't know which is worse, lying here with everyone staring at me or having an ambulance come screaming to the door just to pick me up.*

"Can I-*hweeh*-walk-*hweeh*-in, please?" she asked when the ambulance arrived.

"OK," Mrs. Lorentz agreed. "Angelina, let's help her." Walking between her friend and the nurse made Merrie feel

like the inside of a sandwich.

"I hope you feel better soon," Angelina said. Merrie could tell how worried she was. *She looks almost as bad as I probably do!* She squeezed Angelina's hand and smiled.

Hweeh-hweeh-hweeh-hweeh.

"A little trouble breathing, huh?" the emergency technician said. "Well, let's see if this oxygen helps." He slipped a mask over her mouth. Right away, it helped. By the time they got to the hospital, Merrie was feeling better. After a dose of asthma medicine, she felt much better.

"Can I-*hweeh*-get up-*hwooh*-?" she asked.

"Just lie still until your mother arrives," the nurse said.

Merrie sighed and stared at the ceiling. *Hweeh-hwooh*, she breathed. *Breathe in, breathe out*, she thought.

Finally, she heard her mother's voice answering the nurse's questions. "Yes. Yes, I understand. I'm sure she'll do better." Then Mom appeared beside her.

"Hi, sweetheart. How are you feeling?"

"Fine," Merrie answered. "Can we go?"

In the car, Mom wanted more answers. "What happened? Did this attack come on faster than usual?"

Merrie ducked her head. "No. I could tell it was getting harder to breathe. But you should have seen me—I was playing great! I just didn't want to stop. Mom, I'm tired of being different!"

Her mother smiled sadly. "Merrie, you're like your friends in most ways—and you're smart and cute besides."

"Mom!"

"Sorry. But the truth is, part of you is different. I'm sorry, but it's true, and there's nothing you or I can do about it. You've got to accept that. You have asthma. You may not always have it, but you have it today."

Hweeh-hwooh. "No one else in my class has to stop because they can't breathe." Merrie was starting to get mad. "It's not fair!"

"I know it isn't. But life isn't fair sometimes. Some people are smarter than others—that's not fair. Some people have a talent for music, and some don't—that's not fair. You can paint and draw better than anyone in your class—is that fair?"

Merrie didn't know what to say.

"Life isn't fair, Merrie. But it doesn't help to get mad about it. Just like it doesn't help to pretend you don't have asthma. You'll still have trouble breathing, and if you keep going, you'll still get sick. And all your friends will get scared and worried."

Merrie remembered Angelina's face. "I guess you're right."

"I'm not saying that you shouldn't play or that you can't play hard. You just have to pay attention and know when to stop. Otherwise, you're going to be on the floor with people staring at you again and again."

Merrie made a face. "I don't want that. I'll be more careful, Mom. I promise."

"Good," Mom said. "It may not be fair for me to have a daughter as special as you are, but I still want to keep you."

"Mom!" Merrie rolled her eyes, but she was smiling.

Breathe In, Breathe Out

FAMILY MATTERS

L et's turn to 'Amazing Grace' and stand together to sing."
Wendy stood with everyone else in the church, but she
didn't open her songbook. She was too busy looking
around. It was the most amazing church she had ever
been in.

Not really the church itself, although the cozy little country church was very different from her big brick church at
home. What was really different about this church were the
people.

Wendy turned and stared at the pews full of people. There
were old grandpas and grandmas, crying babies, teenagers,
mothers and fathers, even a few kids her age. *I can't believe
all these people are related to me,* Wendy thought. *Mom said
that our family was big, but this is enormous!*

This was the first year that Wendy and her parents had
traveled to the big Hobart Family Reunion. Already, she had
met aunts, uncles, cousins, and great-grandparents she had

Assurance of salvation

only seen in pictures before.

Two rows back, her cousin Ariel waved and smiled. Already they had plans to get together at the picnic that afternoon.

The preacher was Wendy's Uncle Joe. *He sure looks different than he did at the airport yesterday,* Wendy thought. She listened closely for a few minutes. Then her attention wandered back to the people sitting around her.

Suddenly, Uncle Joe hit the pulpit with his fist. *Bam!* Wendy jumped, and her eyes got big.

"But no one would listen!" Uncle Joe shouted. "Jesus said, 'Wide is the gate that leads to destruction, and narrow is the way that leads to heaven.' That means you're not going to fit through the gate carrying all your sins. You won't make it with your selfishness and hate, with your anger and your pride."

Wendy almost shriveled up like an old grape. *Why does Uncle Joe look like he's talking right to me?* she wondered.

Uncle Joe kept preaching. "The Bible tells a story about Jesus returning to judge the people of the earth. He divides them as a shepherd divides sheep from goats. The good ones go with Him to heaven, but the bad ones are cast out and rejected."

Wendy felt nervous. *What if I'm not good enough to go to heaven? What if everyone in my family is good except for me?* She didn't hear much more of the sermon. Suddenly, the cozy little church almost seemed scary.

Wendy hardly said a word on the trip out to the lake for the family potluck. "Wendy, why don't you go find Ariel," her mom suggested as they unpacked their food. "I know you wanted to play with her."

"I don't feel like playing," Wendy mumbled. Instead, she went and sat at a picnic table by herself. As she watched, members of the family came by and hugged her mom and dad excitedly.

"Wendy, this is your cousin Edward," Mom said. "And this is your Aunt Martha. You already met Ariel." Ariel waved and smiled.

"Hi," Wendy said softly.

"Wendy, we're going for a hike around the lake before lunch," Aunt Martha said. "Do you want to go with us?"

"I don't think so," Wendy said, staring at the picnic table.

"Oh well, join us if you change your mind," her aunt said. As they walked away, Ariel looked really confused.

Wendy's mom and dad whispered for a moment. Then her dad slid onto the bench beside her. "Is something bothering you, honey? All of a sudden, you don't seem very happy to be here. Did someone say something to make you sad?"

Wendy didn't know how to answer. But just then, Uncle Joe walked up. "Yes," she said suddenly. She stood up and pointed. "He did!"

Everyone stared at Uncle Joe. He looked around for a second, then held up his hands. "OK, I confess. I did it. I stole a bite of potato salad."

Even Wendy had to laugh. Uncle Joe made his way over to the picnic table and sat down across from her. "What's going on with this part of the Hobart family?"

Dad shrugged. "Wendy was just telling us that something you said today made her sad."

"Really?" Uncle Joe asked Wendy. She nodded and looked back down at the table. "What did I say?"

Wendy didn't look up. "You said that only good people would go to heaven. And I don't think I'm good enough."

"Wendy!" Dad broke in. "Of course you're good enough."

"I wasn't good enough to make it in the school choir," Wendy pointed out. "And I wasn't good enough to be on the all-star soccer team."

Uncle Joe rubbed his chin. "Wait a minute. Maybe Wendy's right."

Wendy's heart sank down to her shoes. Her dad started to say something, but Uncle Joe waved him quiet. "Wendy, what are you doing at this reunion? Maybe you're not good enough to be here with the Hobarts."

Wendy's head popped up. "Hey, I'm here because my mom is part of the Hobart family. So I am too."

Uncle Joe looked very serious. "And you think that's all you need to be part of the family?"

Wendy looked at her dad, but he didn't say anything. "I think so," she finally whispered.

Uncle Joe grinned. "You're absolutely right, Wendy. You're a part of the family, and that's all that matters. Now, how do you know whether or not you belong in heaven?"

Wendy's eyes dropped again. "If you're good enough, you get to go there."

Bam! Uncle Joe's fist hit the table. "Wrong!"

Wendy jumped. Her eyes got as big as paper plates. "Wendy, only one kind of person belongs in heaven. The kind who belongs to God's family."

Wendy blinked. "You mean heaven is a family reunion?"

Uncle Joe laughed. "Exactly! Everyone who belongs to God's family will get together there for a real picnic. One that doesn't end. Now, Wendy, people who are a part of God's family are trying to be like Him. They want to be kind and honest and unselfish, as Jesus was."

"I'm not like that all the time," Wendy confessed.

Uncle Joe nodded. "The truth is, neither am I. But every day I try to trust God more and let Him help me act more like His child. Like a member of His family."

Wendy thought for a second. "So, how do I know if I'm in God's family?"

"All you have to do is pray and ask Him to make you His child," Uncle Joe said with twinkling eyes. "It's the thing He likes to do most."

"I've been doing that every night for years," Wendy said with a laugh. Suddenly, the lake seemed like a lovely place. "Hey, I'd better hurry if I'm going on that hike with Ariel. See you later, Uncle Joe. And thanks!"

"Hurry back," Mom called after her. "We'll be ready to eat soon."

"Don't worry," Wendy shouted. "I'm already starving. I won't miss lunch."

Uncle Joe laughed again. "Now, that sounds like a real Hobart."

New Kid in the Fort

Shhh!" Manny whispered. "Keep your head down."

Jake ducked and barely breathed. Between the green leaves on the tree's branches, he could see the turning wheels of two bicycles.

Manny whispered again. "A couple of teenagers rode through here last week on their dirt bikes and tore up my old fort. Glad I wasn't here—they like to chase kids around the woods on their bikes."

Jake's eyes got big, but he didn't say anything. Even though he couldn't see the riders' faces, he could hear their voices.

"This is really nice," one person said. "I never knew these woods were here."

"Oh yeah," the other replied, "these woods were here before this town was. I grew up around here. Back then, kids used to build forts and play games all through the trees. But I guess the only thing kids do now is watch TV or play computer games."

Dealing with prejudice; kindness to animals

Manny snickered behind his hand as the bikes disappeared around a turn in the trail. "I knew they wouldn't see us."

"Zowie!" Jake said. "This is a great fort. How did you find it?"

"I was following a rabbit through the bushes, and it led me here. There was kind of a shallow dip here behind the log, so I filled it with leaves. Now, it's cozy, and no one can find me."

"Do you play here a lot?"

Manny's eyes twinkled. "All the time. See that big fir tree over there?" He pulled a limb back so they could see through the leaves. "That's where Nathan has his new hideout. He doesn't think I know where it is, but I've been hiding here, watching him and his little brother, Brody, for two days."

Jake leaned back against the fallen tree trunk. "This place is way better than my old neighborhood. Boy, am I glad we

moved here—and just in time for summer!"

A rustling sound in the leaves behind him brought Manny's finger to his lips. Jake twisted around just in time to see a girl's head pop up over the top of the trunk. She had brown hair just like Manny's.

"Manny, come quick! Something happened to Shadow!" the girl said. Then she turned and disappeared. Before Jake could say a word, Manny hopped up and followed her.

Jake joined the chase. "Manny, who was that?" he called after his new friend. "Where are you going? And who is Shadow?"

The girl shouted back over her shoulder. "Stick around. You'll find out. Just hurry!"

Manny didn't stop. He waved his arm. "Come on!"

They raced between tree trunks and bushes, jumped over logs, and almost stopped in front of an enormous briar patch. "There's no way we can run through that," Jake panted.

But the girl didn't wait. She dropped down on her hands

and knees and crawled into the briars. Manny followed right behind her. Jake shook his head but bent down and saw that they were following a kind of a tunnel through the thorny vines.

"Zowie! I hope these guys know where they're going." Then he plunged in after them.

The vines had been carefully cut, and Jake wasn't poked at all. He popped out the other side and kept going. Before long, he was following Manny and the girl out into someone's back-yard. "Hey, Manny, are you sure this is OK?" he called before his friend disappeared around the corner of a white-and-brown house.

"Come on!" Manny shouted again.

Jake raced to catch up. Under a tree in the yard of a house across the street, a small crowd of kids had gathered. Jake fol-lowed Manny and then stood on his tiptoes to see.

There on the ground lay a clump of black-and-white feathers. "What is that?" Jake whispered. Manny didn't answer, but the girl with the brown hair did.

"It's Shadow. He's a magpie."

"A what?"

A kid on the other side of the circle rolled his eyes. "It's a bird. You know, mostly black with white across the wings and tail?"

"Give him a break, Nathan," Manny said. "Jake just moved here. He probably never saw a magpie before. What happened to Shadow?"

A little kid spoke up. "I saw him from my window." He pointed to the house behind him. "He was on the ground, and my cat Fluffy was chasing him."

"So Fluffy caught him and killed him?" Manny asked.

"I ran out as fast as I could," the little kid protested. "I chased Fluffy away and called Anna. Then she went to get you."

Jake knelt down to look at the bird. He could see that one wing was broken and many feathers were missing. "Whose bird is this?" he asked suddenly.

"What do you mean, whose bird?" Nathan asked. "It doesn't belong to anyone. It just hangs around the neighborhood, pestering people and getting into trash. Like Leonard always said, 'Magpies are just pigs with wings.'"

"Yeah," the little boy next to Nathan added, "Leonard said that the only good magpie was a dead one. Right, Nathan?"

Everyone was quiet for a moment. Jake kept examining the still bird.

Then Anna spoke up. "I don't care what you or Leonard say, Brody. I like magpies. And I'm going to miss having Shadow follow me around begging for food."

Brody laughed. "I bet Fluffy won't miss him. He used to fly down and eat food from Fluffy's bowl. So Fluffy decided to eat him!"

Suddenly, Jake reached down and scooped the bird up with both hands. "Ugh, gross," Nathan said, as everyone backed away. "Put that dead thing down."

"It's not dead," Jake said. "He's still breathing."

"What? Are you sure?" Everyone closed in again.

Jake turned away. "We have to get him to the vet. Manny, is your house near? Will your mom take us?"

Manny pointed back at the white-and-brown house. "We live there. But my mom won't spend any money taking a bird to the vet. She'll say there are lots more where he came from."

Anna nodded, along with most of the other kids. "No one would spend any money saving a magpie," Nathan said.

"Well, my mother will," Jake said. He dashed down the street toward home, holding the bird carefully. He was shouting before he even got to the front door of his house. "Mom! Mom, come quick!"

It only took a minute for Jake's mother to see the problem and grab her purse. As they drove back by, Jake saw that Nathan and Brody and the other kids were still under the tree. But Manny and Anna were across the street in their own yard.

I wonder why Manny hasn't shown Nathan his fort. I wonder if they play together at all. Then the bird stirred in his lap.

"Hurry, Mom. I think he's waking up."

who Shot Shadow?

r. Morgan led Jake and his mother into the office after he had spent some time with the bird. "Well, there's good news and bad news," he said.

"The good news is, the magpie will live. And that surprises me. Usually, just the shock of being handled by humans and being held captive will keep a wild bird from recovering from the injury."

"He's kind of a neighborhood pet," Jake explained. "He's been following the kids around since spring, begging for food. He seems to like people."

"That would explain it," Dr. Morgan agreed. "Well, he was mauled by that cat, and he's still in a little shock, but those wounds will heal. He would be fine if someone hadn't shot his wing."

"Shot him? Zowie! Are you sure?"

The vet nodded. "Probably a BB gun. When his wing bone shattered, he fell to the ground. Then the cat caught him."

Dealing with prejudice; kindness to animals

Jake let out a big breath. "What's the bad news?"

Dr. Morgan sighed. "Knowing that he's been kind of a pet to the children makes this even worse. The broken wing will never heal properly, so the bird will never be able to fly again. Even if he is fed by people, he won't be able to survive in the wild. We'll have to put the bird to sleep."

Jake's mouth fell open. "What? You can't do that!"

"Couldn't we take care of it?" Jake's mother asked. "We've raised birds before—parakeets and parrots."

"You have a cage? A big one?"

Jake jumped up and held his hand up as high as his head. "It's this big. We had it for my parrot, Gomez."

Dr. Morgan looked at Jake for a moment. "Usually, I wouldn't recommend that a wild bird be kept by anyone. But this one is used to humans. We can't set him free, so maybe your cage is the best thing for him."

Jake was still beaming as they drove home with Shadow in a box. "Don't forget what Dr. Morgan told you about caring for that bird," his mother said.

"I won't, Mom. I'm sure other kids will help me."

Jake was hosing out the big cage on his porch when Nathan and Brody walked up. "So, where did you bury the magpie?" Brody asked.

Jake blasted the bottom of the cage. "I didn't. Shadow is alive. He's going to be fine. Except for his wing. He won't ever be able to fly again."

Nathan laughed. "Then Fluffy will have him for lunch before long."

"Nope," Jake replied. "That's what this cage is for. I'm keeping Shadow as a pet."

"Why would anyone want a flying pig for a pet?" Nathan

rolled his eyes.

"I like birds," Jake explained. "I used to have some para-keets. And a parrot."

"A parrot would be cool," Nathan said. "Could yours talk?"

Jake shrugged. "He learned to say a few words. Mostly he just squawked. But I liked having him around." He snapped off the water. "There, that's done. Now it's ready for Shadow."

Shadow inspected his new home carefully, walking from corner to corner. Jake put Shadow's food and water dishes in the cage and brought an extra treat for his new pet.

"Hello, Shadow. Hello, boy." Jake held a peanut out to the bird as he talked. Shadow stuck his beak through the bars of the cage and grabbed it. Holding the peanut in one claw, he jabbed at it until the shell cracked.

Nathan and Brody watched for a minute, then got up. "We have to go," Nathan said. "You wanna go out to the woods tomorrow? I'll show you my fort."

"Sure, that would be great." Jake smiled. *Maybe Nathan wants to be friends after all.* Then he heard another voice.

"Hey, Jake!"

Jake looked up to see Manny and Anna at the edge of his yard. "Is Shadow OK?" Anna called.

"Come and see him yourself."

Anna looked at Manny. "Are you sure it's OK?" Manny asked.

Jake waved his arm. "Why wouldn't it be? Come on." They raced across the yard and up the steps.

"Look! He's hopping around and everything!" Anna was delighted to see the bird.

Manny was grinning too. "He looks a little ragged without those feathers. How long until you can let him go?"

Jake frowned. "That's the bad news. His wing was . . . broken, and the vet says Shadow will never be able to fly. But the good news is—he gets to stay with me!"

"You're going to keep him? Right here in this cage?" By the look on Anna's face, Jake knew she liked that idea.

"Will Shadow let you touch him?" Manny asked.

"He lets me touch him," Jake said. "I don't know if he'll let anyone else yet. But he'll take a peanut from your fingers if you hold it out."

They took turns giving Shadow peanuts for a few minutes. Then Jake asked, "Where have you guys been? I thought you'd be waiting when I got back."

"We've had a few problems of our own," Manny said.

"Someone shot a hole in Manny's bedroom window with a BB gun," Anna explained. "We've been trying to figure out who did it."

Jake sat up straight. "Zowie! With a BB gun? Are you sure?"

Manny nodded.

"So who did it?" Jake asked.

"We're not sure," Manny answered. "But I know two kids

on this street who have BB guns."

Jake frowned. "I haven't told anyone else about this, but I think I can trust you two. I know you didn't do it because you were with me."

"Do what?" Manny asked.

"Shadow was shot by a BB gun. That's how his wing was broken. Fluffy must have found him on the ground."

Anna's brown eyes got big. Manny's mouth fell open.

"So," Jake went on, "whoever shot your window must have shot Shadow too. Which kids on the block have a BB gun?"

Manny took a breath. "Carlos has one. He lives in that brick house on the corner. But I haven't seen him around much this summer."

"Nathan has one too," Anna added. "He got it on his birthday last spring. He showed it off to everyone."

I wonder if Nathan did it, Jake thought. *I know he doesn't like magpies—and he doesn't seem to like Manny.* Out loud he said, "Let's not tell anyone about Shadow until we figure out who's doing the shooting."

Those Kinds of People

As the summer went by, Jake spent a lot of time with Shadow. Now the bird would follow him around the yard whenever Jake let him out of his cage.

Jake also spent a lot of time playing with Nathan and Manny—but never at the same time. If he was with Manny and Anna, Nathan had other things to do. If he was hanging around with Nathan, Manny never showed up.

One day he was sitting in his yard with Shadow. "Hello, Shadow. Hello," he said as the bird stood on his shoulder.

"Squaak," Shadow answered, begging for more food.

"Hey, Jake," Manny called as he and Anna walked up, "it happened again."

"What happened? Not another magpie hurt, I hope."

"No," Anna answered. "But something else was shot with a BB gun. Our back porch light has a little hole right through it."

Jake frowned. "Zowie. And no one saw who did it, right?

Dealing with prejudice; kindness to animals

Well, we know it wasn't Carlos this time."

"Nope. He's gone to his grandparents' house for the summer," Manny said. "So who did it?"

Anna spoke up. "I still think Nathan is doing it."

"But I told you that he said his mother took away his BB gun for the summer," Jake protested.

"I know," Anna said, "because he got bad grades. But what if he's lying about that, just so we won't suspect him?"

Jake looked at them both. "Why don't you guys ever play with Nathan? You must have had a fight or something. He won't even go near your house—and you never go to his."

"We don't go to anyone's house unless they invite us," Anna said.

"That's true," Jake remembered. "You almost wouldn't come to my house at first. But why? And what's the deal with Nathan?"

Manny shrugged. "He doesn't like us."

"Why?"

Anna answered. "Stick around. You'll find out."

She was right. A few days later, Jake found out without even asking.

He was following Nathan and Brody to their fort. "Hey, aren't we going the long way around?" he asked as they took a different trail through the woods.

"Yeah," Nathan said, "but we go this way to get around that big briar patch behind Manny's house."

Jake was confused. "But there's a path through—"

Brody interrupted him. "We don't go by some people's yards."

"Yeah, I know." Jake was going to ask more, but Nathan stopped and held up his hand. "Did you hear something?" He pointed toward the fort.

"Is it those dirt bikers?" Brody whispered. "C'mon, let's go!"

The three boys crept along as quietly as possible, dodging to stay out of sight of anyone who might be on the bike trail. They heard the roar of a motorcycle, but it could have been far away.

"Good," Nathan said as they got closer to the fort, "we don't have to worry about them today."

They walked near Manny's fort, but Nathan didn't say anything. In fact, with the thick leaves there, he couldn't even see the tree trunk lying on the ground.

But Nathan saw something. Not at Manny's fort—at his. "Oh, great! Look what someone did!"

They raced forward to see that the limbs of the fir tree had been broken or twisted back. Nathan's fort was destroyed. Two books and some pop cans lay scattered on the ground, along with a small hatchet.

"Zowie," Jake said quietly.

"Those dirt-bike jerks!" Brody shouted. "I'd like to—"

"Stop shouting," Nathan commanded. Jake could see that he was steaming mad. "We don't know for sure that those bikers did it. It could have been someone else. Like Manny."

Jake wasn't sure he heard right. "Are you kidding? Manny wouldn't do something like this."

"How would you know?" Nathan demanded. "You've only lived here a few weeks." He picked up the books. "Leonard always said, you just can't trust those people. I guess he was right."

Jake still didn't understand. "Who is this Leonard guy you're always talking about?"

"A kid who used to live in your house—before you moved here," Nathan explained. "He was always telling jokes and making everyone laugh. We used to build forts together and stuff like that."

"And Leonard said you shouldn't trust Manny?"

Nathan bristled. "Hey, Leonard knew a lot of stuff. He was older than me or you."

Jake shook his head. *Maybe this Leonard guy knew something about Manny that I don't know,* he thought. "So, what did Leonard tell you?"

Nathan turned to stare. "Do I have to draw a picture for you? You can't trust Mexicans—people with brown skin and

Those Kinds of People

black hair, like Manny and his family. They're lazy and dumb, and they're liars. You can't trust 'em."

Jake could hardly believe his ears. "That's it? You don't like them because they look different than you? That's crazy!"

"No!" Nathan shouted, "you're the one whose crazy for hanging around with him all the time. He probably tore up my fort because you've been playing with me. So you're going to have to decide—if you play with Mexicans, you're not playing with us."

Jake just stood there while Nathan and Brody picked up their stuff. Shaking his head, he turned to stare at the spot where the big tree trunk was lying on the ground. *I wonder if Manny is back there right now, listening to this.*

Is there any way Nathan could be right?

Under the Skin

12

Jake stomped into the house, still upset. "Mom, can I ask you something?"

"Just a minute, Jake. I'm on the phone."

Jake wandered into the kitchen and spread peanut butter on a slice of bread while he waited. His mother came in on the third bite. "So, what's up?"

"Natha dothnt kike Mana becawt—"

"Jake! Finish chewing your food first." She waited until he swallowed.

"Nathan doesn't like Manny because he's a Mexican. He says that all Mexicans are dumb and lazy and that they're liars."

His mom didn't blink. "So, is he right?"

Jake was confused again. "Mom! You're supposed to tell me. I don't know any Mexican people."

"You know Manny," she insisted. "Is he?"

Jake stopped to think. "Manny has the best fort in the woods. He was smart enough to find a great spot and worked

Dealing with prejudice; kindness to animals

Under the Skin

hard to make it even better. And he's never lied to me, as far as I know. He and Anna care about Shadow. I like them."

"OK, then," Mom said, "you know Nathan is wrong about Manny. I don't think he's right about other Mexicans, either. Jake, there are some Mexican people who are lazy and some who lie. But there are plenty of people who look like you and me who do the same things."

Jake chewed another bite of his peanut-butter bread. Mom went on. "People are not good or bad because of the color of their skin or the way they look. What matters is what's under the skin—their hearts. If Manny has a good heart, be his friend."

By the time Jake was through with his snack, he had decided what to do next. He wasn't a bit nervous until he rang the door-bell at the brown-and-white house down the street. "Manny will be glad to see us—right, Shadow?"

"Squaak," Shadow said quietly.

A woman opened the door. "Yes?" she asked, with a puzzled look on her face.

"Hi! I'm Jake. Is Manny home?"

She lifted one eyebrow and almost smiled. "Oh, you are the bird boy, yes?" Then she got serious. "Is there some kind of trouble?"

"No, I just wanted to see if Manny could play," Jake answered.

Her face lighted with a big smile. "Come in! Come in!

Manuel, your friend is here," she called into the next room.

Manny and Anna both rushed in. And they were both surprised to see Jake in their own living room. "What are you

doing here?" Manny asked.

"You came to my house," Jake teased. "Can't I come to yours?"

Manny's answer was a big smile. Anna said, "Anytime—as long as you bring Shadow." She showed the bird off to the rest of the family, then handed him back to Jake when they headed out to the fort.

Shadow squawked as they crawled through the briar patch, but he kept quiet when they tiptoed through the trees and snuck into their fort. Manny took one look through the leaves and hissed, "Hey, what happened to Nathan's fort? Was it those teenage dirt bikers?"

"Nathan thinks it might have been," Jake answered with a

shrug. "They tore it all up."

"I'm glad they didn't find ours," Anna said. "Hey, wait a minute! Manny, didn't we see them on the bike trail last summer, shooting a BB gun?"

"That's right! They're probably the ones who shot you, Shadow."

Jake nodded. "And your house. Come on. Let's make sure they can't find our fort."

They hadn't worked long when Anna's watch alarm beeped. "It's my turn to help my mother with supper," she said. "See you later."

"What're you cooking?" Jake called after her teasingly.

"Stick around. You'll find out."

Not long after Anna left, Jake heard footsteps in the leaves. "Shh!" he hissed. "Someone's coming." They both ducked down and peered through the leaves.

It was Nathan. He was carrying his little hatchet and a rake. He set them down near the bike trail and wandered back and forth, looking at trees and bushes. "He must be looking for a place to build a new fort," Manny whispered.

Sitting there watching Nathan, Jake felt a little weird. *I could be out there helping him,* he thought. Then he argued with himself. *But it's Nathan's fault. He said I couldn't be friends with him and Manny too. And no one's going to tell me who I can be friends with.*

Manny interrupted his thinking. "Do you hear that?" Jake listened, and he heard it too. The sound of motorcycles. And they were getting closer.

A few seconds later, two dirt bikes roared around a curve in the trail. They whipped by Jake and Manny and slid to a stop in front of Nathan.

"Hey, kid," one biker called as the bikes grumbled quietly, "was that your fort we accidently ran into yesterday?" He laughed and twisted the red baseball cap on his head.

"Yeah, you jerks," Nathan answered. He was still mad. "Why don't you leave kids alone?"

"Oh, the little guy's mad," the other biker said. He flipped his ponytail back and forth. "Maybe we should run into something else. Like you." With that, Ponytail released the clutch, and his bike leapt forward, almost onto Nathan's foot.

"Hey, stop it!" Nathan shouted as he backed away. But Red Cap joined in. He roared his bike up beside Nathan and reached out to shove him.

Jake heard Manny mumble something, but he didn't turn. *Come on, Nathan,* he was thinking. *Get away from them!*

Almost as if he had heard Jake's thought, Nathan turned to run. But after only a few steps, he tripped on a root and went sprawling onto the ground.

Jake could just see the bikers riding right over Nathan's body. And laughing. *Zowie! We've got to help Nathan! But how?*

Enemies and Friends

13

We've got to do something," Jake whispered. But Manny was already doing it. He was running straight at the teenagers. "Pick on someone your own size!" he shouted as he ran up to the one with the ponytail.

"Hey, another one!" Ponytail snorted. "Let's get him!" The

back tire sprayed dirt as he took off through the trees after Manny. Red Cap was right behind him.

Jake ran over to Nathan. "Are you OK?"

"I tripped on that root and

Dealing with prejudice; kindness to animals

twisted my ankle," Nathan moaned. "Is Manny crazy? They'll get him for sure."

"Don't be too sure. I think I know where he's headed. Here, hold Shadow. I'm going to help Manny."

Jake raced through the woods after the two bikers. They were closing in on Manny now. Suddenly, Manny went down. "We got him now!" Red Cap shouted.

But Manny hadn't fallen. He dove into the tunnel through the briar patch. Both bikers slammed on their brakes. "Come on. Follow me in here!" Manny taunted them.

Before they could get off their bikes to chase him, Jake ran up behind Red Cap. "Chase someone your own size!" he shouted. Then he turned and ran as fast as he could back toward Manny's fort.

Just from the sound of the motorcycles, he could tell they were chasing him. And getting closer every second. *This plan better work!* he thought. Then he dove through the bushes into the fort.

Hidden under the bushes was the fallen tree trunk. Jake knew that. The bikers didn't.

Crash! Red Cap hit the log. "Oww!" He flew off onto the ground.

Crash! Ponytail hit Red Cap's bike. "Whoa!" He flew on top of Red Cap.

Jake lay still and kept quiet. He hoped Manny and Nathan would do the same.

"Get off me," Red Cap shouted. "Oh, man, look at my bike. My dad's going to kill me. Come on. Let's go."

"But what about those kids?" Ponytail asked.

"Who cares about them? Look at my bike!"

Jake waited until the voices were farther away, then stuck

his head up. "Are you guys OK?" he called.

"No problems here," Manny answered as he came out of the briar patch. "Good trick. They won't be buzzing through these woods for a while."

"I'm OK," Nathan added. "Thanks to you guys."

Jake flopped down near Nathan. "Zowie! That was really something."

"Zowie!"

Jake looked up. Nathan's eyes looked as if they were going to pop out. Manny's mouth was hanging open. "Who said that?" Jake asked. Before anyone could answer, it was said again.

"Zowie! Hello, hello."

"Shadow can talk!" Nathan could hardly believe his ears.

"How did you teach him to do that?" Manny wanted to know.

Jake just laughed. "I wanted to show Nathan that magpies are more than 'pigs with wings.' Then I found out that they're mimics—like crows and jays. And they can be trained to talk. So I've been trying to teach Shadow like I taught my parrot. But this is the first time he ever said anything!"

Nathan looked at the bird as though he had never seen it before. "I can't believe it. A magpie talking! I guess Leonard was wrong."

Then Nathan looked up at Manny. "I guess Leonard was wrong about a lot of things. Thanks for helping me. I didn't deserve it—not after the way I've treated you."

Manny put out his hand and helped Nathan up. "It was nothing. Those two guys couldn't catch a turtle on a race-track. Besides, it was worth it to make a friend."

Just then, the sound of someone crashing through the

trees made them all jump. Jake grabbed Shadow and stood in front of Nathan. But the person who jumped out had a gun!

"Brody! What are you doing?" Nathan pushed past Jake and limped over to his little brother. "And what are you doing with my BB gun?"

Brody was confused. "I heard motorcycles. I thought you might need your gun. Where are those biker guys?"

"Jake and Manny scared them away already," Nathan said. "You know where Mom hid my BB gun?"

"Oh, sure, I found it a long time ago," Brody said. Then he saw Nathan and Manny staring at him. "I mean, I found it yesterday."

Nathan saw the stares too. "What's going on?"

Manny cleared his throat. "Someone's been shooting at my house with a BB gun. They broke our porch light and shot a hole in my window."

"It wasn't me," Brody said quickly. "You're just trying to blame someone. It was probably you—or your sister." He turned to Nathan. "You know them. They always lie. The next thing you know, he'll blame me for shooting Shadow."

Jake stopped with a peanut halfway out of his pocket. "Did you say 'shooting Shadow'? Why would you say that?"

Brody hesitated. Nathan butted in. "Shadow wasn't shot. He was hurt by a cat."

"Well, that's not exactly true, Nathan," Jake said. "At the vet's office, I found out that Shadow's wing was broken by a shot from a BB gun. But no one else knows that except Manny, Anna—and the person who shot him."

Brody looked away. "Brody," Nathan asked, "did you do it?"

Brody threw down the gun. "Yes! Yes, I shot Shadow. The only good magpie is a dead one anyway. I want to shoot them all." He turned to Manny. "And I shot your window and porch light too! Everyone knows that Mexicans are liars and cheats. I wish you would all move away, back to where you belong. Right, Nathan?"

Nathan just stared at the ground.

Brody tried again. "Nathan?"

"Brody, Leonard was wrong about some things. He was wrong about a lot of things."

Brody's eyes got watery. "Nathan, you told me about magpies and Mexicans. It's not fair! It's your fault! I'm telling Mom!" Then he turned and ran toward home.

Nathan started to limp after him. "I guess he learned a lot from me—too much. I'd better go explain. See you guys later."

"Zowie," Jake said under his breath.

"Zowie, zowie," Shadow repeated.

Later, Jake was showing off Shadow's talking to the rest of Manny's family when the doorbell rang. Anna opened the door. There stood Nathan.

"Hi! We're having a picnic tomorrow at my house, and I wanted to invite you all to come."

Manny stepped up beside her. "Close your mouth, Anna. You're attracting flies."

Anna was still in shock. "Will someone please tell me what's going on?"

Jake grinned. "Stick around. You'll find out."

"Zowie!" Shadow added.

Happy to Be Arrested!

Do you like this one?" Evie held up the shirt for her friends to see.

Candace wrinkled her nose. "Too red. I liked the other better."

"It's perfect!" Hayley argued. "I want it."

Evie put the shirt back on the rack. "I'm sure glad you guys came to the mall tonight. I thought I was going to have to sit in the Hair House with nothing to do but watch Mom's hair curl."

"Your mom won't let you walk around?" Candace asked.

Evie shook her head. "Not by myself. She says it's too dangerous. She thinks there are too many weirdos around."

"Moms always think that," Candace said, rolling her eyes.

"Hey," Hayley whispered, "look at that guy's boots."

Both Evie and Candace turned. The man walked over to a rack of coats. As he did, little silver spurs on his boots jingled. He smiled at the girls.

Protection from strangers

"You like spurs?" Candace asked. "I don't even like boots."

"Come on. Let's go," Evie said. They wandered through the mall stores, having a soda at the ice-cream shop and watching the game players at the arcade.

When they stopped at the pet shop, they heard a voice down by the exit. "Candace! Candace, come on."

"It's my mom," Candace said. "I guess we have to go, Hayley. See you later, Evie."

" 'Bye." Evie waved and didn't really think about being alone until she turned to walk away. *Mom would have a fit if she knew I was all alone out here. Oh well, what she doesn't know won't worry her. I'll just walk back to the Hair House.*

Evie turned a corner and headed to the escalator. She loved riding up so she could watch the people below get shorter and farther away. As she neared the top, the man with the silver spurs on his boots stepped on at the bottom.

Someone should tell him that the western store is downstairs, Evie thought as she turned away. Then she had an idea. *I'll stop by that bookstore and get a magazine to read while I wait for Mom.* A few steps down the hall to her right brought her to the open doors of . . . The Furniture Shop?

"Hey, where's the bookstore?" Evie asked out loud. No one answered, so she turned and stared up and down the mall. "I know it was here before," she muttered.

Then she remembered. *It's on the other side of Candy-by-the-Ton. By that craft place, I think.* As she turned to go back past the escalator, she saw that the man with the spurs was looking at the furniture.

After a few more turns, Evie found the craft shop. But the bookstore wasn't there. *Where is it? Where am I?* Suddenly, she felt a little nervous. *I'd better find one of those mall maps.*

She heard footsteps behind her and turned to ask if that person knew where the bookstore was. "Do you—" Then she froze. It was the man with the silver spurs. He was smiling at her, but something about that smile made goose bumps come up on her arms.

Without saying another word, Evie turned and ran down the mall away from him. She ducked into the first store she came to.

Dodging past a display of beautiful glass animals, Evie walked quickly down the aisle. *I think that man is following me! What am I going to do? Oh, Candace and Hayley, come back!*

She stopped beside a rack of birthday cards. Rubbing her arms with both hands, she picked a card. But she was too nervous to even see the words. Then she heard a sound that made her almost stop breathing.

Jingle, jingle. The man with the spurs walked in.

He really is following me! What am I going to do?

Without even looking back, Evie ducked down the farthest aisle and walked quickly to the end. There, behind a rack of doll clothes, she tried to think. *What did Mother say I should*

Happy to be Arrested!

do if I'm in danger? Look for a police officer or an adult in charge. But there's no one around except him!

Then she heard it again. The *jingle, jingle* sound was getting closer. She peeked down the aisle. He was coming right toward her!

Just then, a woman in a blue uniform grabbed Evie's shoulder from behind. "Hold it right there," she said. "I'm the security guard here," the woman said, "and I'm going to arrest you for shoplifting."

Evie almost fainted. "But—I didn't—but . . ."

"Where are your parents?" the woman demanded.

"My mom's at . . ." Evie started to answer, but the security officer wasn't even looking at her. "Was that man following you?" she asked quietly.

Evie could only nod her head.

The woman patted her arm. "I thought so. Just a moment." She held up a radio and spoke into it. "Security, this is Pam in Crystal Palace. We have a possible abduction attempt. Male, medium height, wearing boots with silver spurs."

After answering a few questions, she turned back to Evie. "Are you OK?"

Evie nodded. "Where did you come from? I thought I was alone."

"That big mirror at the end is really a security door. I was watching you. Then I popped out and grabbed you."

"I really didn't steal anything," Evie said.

Pam laughed. "Oh, I know that. I just said that to scare him off."

Evie was confused. "What?"

"I was watching you through the security mirrors, and I thought you were scared. But I didn't know if he was the

problem. I figured I'd come out and arrest you for shoplifting. If he was your dad or something, he'd come right over. If he wasn't, he'd take off. Just like he did."

Happy to be Arrested!

Evie started to relax. "Thanks. I've never seen that man before tonight, but he's been following me for a long way."

Pam frowned. "If you're ever caught all alone like that again and someone is scaring you, the best thing to do is scream. As loud as you can. That will get everyone's attention, and the bad person will usually leave."

"I can do that," Evie decided.

"Great. Now, where are your parents?"

Evie's eyes got big. "My mom's down at the Hair House. She's probably having a fit worrying about me."

"Come on," Pam said. "I'll take you there."

"Wait until I tell her how I was arrested for shoplifting," Evie said with a laugh. "She'll be so happy!"

Proud of It

Justin knew it would be a long ride home even before he got in the car. He had seen enough of the looks from where his parents were sitting across the church. *Come on,* he said to himself. *Get it over with.*

His dad didn't wait long. "Justin, I'm disappointed in the way you acted in church today."

"Aw, Dad, I wasn't doing anything."

Mom turned to stare at him. "Justin, you and Andy were laughing and punching each other during the songs. And you talked and scuffled during Pastor Glenn's sermon. You weren't being reverent at all."

Justin rolled his eyes. "What difference does it make how I was acting?"

Dad tried to explain. "Justin, reverence for God during worship is important. It shows on the outside how you feel on the inside about God."

"Everyone there knows that I'm a Christian and I love

Reverence

God," Justin insisted. "And I was listening most of the time—except during the boring parts."

"Everyone there loves God. Why do you think they were all sitting quietly during the sermon?" Mom asked.

Justin knew it was the wrong answer, but he said it anyway. "Because they were tired?"

Dad frowned in the rearview mirror. "Justin, plan on sitting with us in church from now on."

"Fine," Justin answered. He fell back against the car seat and folded his arms. *I still don't know what the big deal is,* he thought.

That evening, Dad looked at Justin over the top of his newspaper. "Hey, you feel like going to the hockey game tomorrow night?"

"Yes!" Justin shouted. Then he calmed down. "I'd love to go." Hockey was his favorite sport, and the Avengers were his favorite team.

The next evening found Justin and his dad winding their

way through the crowds. "What seats do we have?" Dad asked.

Justin checked the tickets. "Section C, Row 14, Seat 7 and Seat 8. Good seats this time." They wound their way to those seats, collecting some popcorn and drinks along the way.

"This is great," Justin shouted to his dad. He had to shout to be heard above the noise of the crowd and the music. Dad just smiled. Finally, they started announcing the team members. Justin shouted with everyone else.

Then everything got quiet. Justin felt goose bumps on his skin. This was one of his favorite parts. The game was about to start, but before the whistle blew, everyone would stand for the national anthem.

Nothing made Justin prouder than standing beside his father during the national anthem. People said they could tell that his father had been in the army. "He has a lot of love and respect for his country. You can see it in the way he stands so straight with his hand over his heart. And the way he salutes the raised flag as the song ends."

It made Justin feel proud of his father and proud of his country. And he wanted everyone to know it.

"Ladies and gentlemen, your national anthem."

Justin stood with everyone else and put his hand over his heart. He turned to smile at his dad and nearly fell over in shock.

His dad was still sitting down! He was just sitting there, reading the game program.

"Dad!" Justin grabbed at his dad's arm. "Come on! Stand up!" Dad just waved him away and kept reading. Justin felt his face get red. The man in front of them turned around and frowned. A woman behind them was whispering and pointing.

Proud of It

What is wrong with him? Justin tried to figure it out. Not sure what else to do, Justin sat down too.

Dad looked at him and smiled. "So, do you think the Avengers will win tonight?" he asked in a loud voice. Several other people turned to stare.

Justin felt like crawling under the seat. "Dad! What are you doing? Everyone thinks you're being disrespectful of your country—that you don't care about it."

"You don't think that, do you?" Dad asked. "I mean, you know I served my country. You know how important it is to me."

"Yes," Justin admitted. "But—"

Dad interrupted. "Then it doesn't really matter how I act, does it? If this is the boring part to me, then I should be able to do something else, right?"

Justin opened his mouth, but nothing came out. *Uh-oh,* he thought. *That sounds like something I said yesterday.* He just sat there until the song ended.

Then his dad jumped up. "Come on," he said, grabbing Justin's arm. "You're going to miss the face-off."

When the puck dropped, Justin forgot about his dad's strange behavior and got into the game. "Go, go, go!" he shouted with everyone else as a wingman broke away for a one on one with the goalie.

The flashing light lit up three times for each team, and the score was tied at the last minute. Then the Avenger center slapped a shot that slipped in over the goalie's outstretched glove and hit the net.

"Yaay!" Justin screamed with the crowd. "We win! We win!"

The whole way back to the car, Justin dashed back and forth, practicing pretend shots on goal. But on the way home,

he started thinking again.

"Dad, is reverence like respect?"

"Yes, it is, Justin."

"You were trying to teach me something when you didn't pay attention to the national anthem, weren't you?" Dad smiled and nodded. Justin made a face. "It did matter to me that you weren't showing respect. I was worried about you, and I was embarrassed. Is that how you and Mom felt at church?"

Dad nodded again. "We did. But it's more than just that. Just standing during the national anthem doesn't prove that you love your country. But if you do love it, then standing is something you really want to do."

"I get it," Justin said. "Being quiet and reverent in church doesn't prove that you love God. But if you really do love Him, being reverent is something you really want to do."

Dad reached over and patted Justin's leg. "If you're proud to be a Christian, it shows—not just when you're at school or

110

at the park or when you're helping someone, but when you're in church too."

"Got it, Dad. I'll try to sit quietly during worship next week."

Dad laughed. "OK. I'll try not to sit during the national anthem the next time we go to a game."

"It's a deal."

No Friends Again

This year is going to be different, Chelley promised herself as she walked up the stairway to her first class. *This year, I'm going to make friends.* After walking up three flights, she checked her notebook to be sure she knew the right room number. "Three fifteen," she mumbled. Then she walked to the door with that number over it.

The first thing she did was bump into a tall red-haired girl. "Sorry," Chelley mumbled, staring at the floor.

The girl shook her head. "My fault. I guess I look like a door," she called over her shoulder to the other kids. They all laughed. Chelley slunk over to an empty desk and tried to disappear.

"All right, let's settle down," the teacher said as she walked in. "My name is Mrs. Yount, and this is your homeroom. This is where you will come first every morning, and I'll be your teacher for science and social studies. Now, let's see who's here. Please tell me if I pronounce your name wrong."

> **Shyness; making friends;
> being an example**

Chelley slumped down farther. *Oh, please get it right!* she said silently to the teacher. Before long, the teacher reached her name. "Chelley?" she said as if it started with the same sound as *church*.

Chelley turned red. "It's pronounced Shelley."

Mrs. Yount looked at her with a smile. "Chelley," she said correctly. "OK. Andrea?"

"Here," the red-haired girl answered. "Is it time for recess yet?" Everyone laughed, and Mrs. Yount smiled.

"Not yet," she answered. "Chris?" There was no answer. "Chris?" she asked again. Finally, a boy near the back spun around in his seat.

"Here!" he almost shouted. Everyone laughed again. "Sorry," he mumbled.

"Please stop talking and pay attention, Chris," Mrs. Yount said. "Steven?"

The boy right behind Chris waved his hand. "Here," he called. "I'm here, Mrs. Yount. And I'm paying attention." Everyone laughed except Chris.

"Hey, Steven was the one talking to me," he protested.

Mrs. Yount just said, "Today, you have chosen where you want to sit. If necessary, I'll choose a different seat for you." Then she went on calling the role.

Why can't you be loud and friendly like those kids? Chelley said to herself. *Everyone will want to be friends with Andrea*

No Friends Again

and Chris and Steven. But Chelley knew she couldn't. If she tried to say something funny, it would sound dumb. And everyone would stare at her like she should be in a cage at the zoo.

"I'd like to introduce one other member of our class," Mrs. Yount said as she finished. She walked to the side of the classroom by the windows. "This is Morey. He's our class hamster."

"Ahh," Chelley moaned. She loved animals. *He looks soft like Benjamin,* she thought, comparing him to her pet rabbit. *I wonder if I can help take care of him.*

Mrs. Yount answered her question. "We'll all take turns taking care of Morey. Each day, one member of the class will be assigned to give him his food and water."

Andrea raised her hand and waved. "Mrs. Yount, can I take care of him first?"

"May I, Andrea," Mrs. Yount said. "May I take care of him."

Andrea looked confused. "You're the teacher. You can take care of him if you want to."

Chelley understood. She almost turned red just thinking about how embarrassed she would be to make that mistake. As she looked around, Chelley looked at a girl who had answered to the name of Caitlin. Caitlin's eyebrows went up. She understood it too.

Mrs. Yount explained. "Andrea, you should say, 'May I take care of Morey,' not 'Can I.' You're asking permission, not asking if you are able. And yes, Andrea, you may."

Chelley turned to see what color Andrea was turning. Everyone was staring. And laughing. But Andrea was laughing too. *She's not even embarrassed! I would have died! I must*

be the Red Face Champion of the World.

As Mrs. Yount gave them their first assignment, Chelley looked over at Caitlin again. *She seems like a friendly person. I wish I could make friends with her.* But inside, Chelley knew it wouldn't happen. This year was going to be just like all those years at her old school.

That next morning, Chelley almost tripped over two suitcases by the front door. "Hey, who's moving out?" she called.

"It's me," her dad answered from the kitchen. "But I'm not moving. I'm leaving on another business trip this morning."

Chelley came and leaned over his shoulder to look at his newspaper. "What do you do on all these trips, Dad?"

He reached up and patted her head. "You know I sell computer programs. I'm traveling to meet with someone who might want to buy some."

Chelley shuddered. "I couldn't do your job—traveling around talking to strangers—I just couldn't."

"It's not so bad, Chelley. They aren't strangers for long. I try to turn them into friends."

"How do you do that so fast, Dad?"

He turned another page of his newspaper as he answered. "It's

No Friends Again

pretty simple, really. You just get them to talk about them-selves. Almost everyone likes to talk about their families or their business—anything about themselves. By paying atten-tion when they talk and not interrupting, you make them feel special and important."

Chelley raised one eyebrow. "And that works?"

"Hey," her dad answered, "that's what's paying for this house. I make friends like that. Then I make money by selling them the things they need."

Chelley hugged him. "You're the greatest," she said. "The great-est salesman—and the greatest dad."

"OK, OK," he said, finally unwrapping from her arms. "Let me finish reading the basketball scores."

"Dad," Chelley protested, "you don't even like basketball."

"No," he admit-ted, "but my cus-tomer tomorrow does. And this will give me another thing to talk to him about. Hey, you'd better get going, or you'll miss your bus."

She hugged him again. "I'll miss you."

"Not for long. I'll be back tomorrow night. Have a good day at school, sweetheart."

On the way to school, Chelley kept thinking. *I wonder if I could use Dad's tricks to make friends with Caitlin?* But when she got to her classroom, the thought disappeared.

Even before she got to the door, she could hear kids shouting and laughing. Then she heard a voice. "Shh! I think she's coming!"

As Chelley stepped up to the classroom door, everyone was silent.

Shouting Silently

17

Chelley fought the urge to turn and run back down the stairs. She leaned forward and poked her head in the room.

"That's not Mrs. Yount, you chicken," Chris called. He and Steven ran to the front of the room and bent down behind the teacher's desk.

With everyone ignoring her, Chelley walked happily and quickly to her desk. She heard Andrea's voice. "Mrs. Yount is going to have a fit when she sits down. And if she falls over, you guys are going straight to the principals's office."

From listening, Chelley learned that Chris and Steven were unscrewing one of the rollers on Mrs. Yount's chair. Caitlin was shaking

Shyness; making friends; being an example

her head. "What if she falls over and gets hurt?" she asked someone sitting next to her.

Chelley didn't like it either. *Someone should tell Mrs. Yount,* she decided. But when the teacher came in, Chelley was quiet along with everyone else. *Don't sit down!* she shouted silently. But Mrs. Yount did.

Almost. At the last minute, she reached down to roll the chair farther from the desk. With a loud *clunk*, it tipped up. Everyone was even quieter as she looked up. "It seems that a wheel has fallen off my chair," she said finally. "Can I have two volunteers to put it back on? How about you, Chris? And Steven? Thank you."

The rest of the class time went by quietly until Mrs. Yount announced a science project. "As we study gravity and motion, we are going to have a contest. I'm going to divide our class into teams of two. And I want each team to drop a fresh egg from our classroom window and have it fall to the ground without breaking."

The whole class started buzzing. "You can't do that! It's impossible. You couldn't throw a rock from there without breaking it."

"Now, wait a minute," Mrs. Yount interrupted. "I want you to find a way to counteract the force of gravity. Give your egg a parachute. Build a cushion around it. Do whatever you think will keep it from breaking. Next week at this time, we'll be throwing our eggs out the window."

To Chelley's delight, Mrs. Yount assigned her and Caitlin as partners. They moved their desks together. "Hi," Caitlin said. "Do you really think it's possible to keep our egg from breaking?"

Chelley hesitated. "I guess it must be. Mrs. Yount thinks it will work." She could feel her face getting hot. *What did Dad say he did?* Then she remembered. "Have you lived here a long time? My family just moved to this school district."

Caitlin nodded. "I've lived near here since I was born. I went to school with most of these kids last year." She thought for a second. "But my sister went here two years ago. She had Mrs. Yount. Maybe she remembers how they did the egg thing. I'll ask her tonight."

Chelley beamed and tried to remember what to do next.

"Do you have just one sister?" she asked as they opened their science books. Then she listened as Caitlin talked about her sisters and her home on a ranch. When science was over, Chelley knew more about Caitlin than she did about gravity and motion. But that didn't bother her.

Maybe I can really make a friend, Chelley thought as she walked home from the bus stop. *What else did Dad say he does?* As soon as she walked in the door, she called, "Dad! Dad, are you home?"

Her mother stuck her head into the room. "He left on his

trip this morning, remember?"

"Oh yeah." Then Chelley remembered something else. "Mom, don't we have a book about horses?"

Her mother sounded surprised. "Horses? What is it, a report you have to do? I know you don't like horses."

"Mom! It's not for me. It's for a friend—I hope."

Later that week, Chelley hesitated at the door to her class-room. The buzzing sound of kids talking fast and loud almost frightened her. But as she stepped in, no one paid any attention. She was relieved that Chris and Steven weren't doing anything to Mrs. Yount's desk.

But several boys, including those two, were huddled around the hamster cage. While Chelley watched, Andrea ran back to where they were.

"I wonder what they're up to now," Caitlin called from her desk. "Some dumb trick, probably. Hey, Andrea, what are they going to do?"

Chelley listened as Andrea came up to Caitlin's desk. "They're planning another trick on Mrs. Yount," Andrea reported. "When we pack up our eggs and drop them out the window, Mrs. Yount is going to be down on the ground to see if they broke."

"Right," Caitlin agreed. "One of us has to drop the egg, and the other has to be down with Mrs. Yount. So?"

"Well, Chris and Steven are building a parachute to float their egg down. Only they're not going to drop an egg— they're going to hook the hamster up to their parachute!"

Chelly gasped. *They can't do that!* she shouted silently.

Caitlin was thinking the same thing. "Hey, what if Morey gets hurt?"

Andrea shrugged. "You know those two—if they think it'll be funny and shock the teacher, they'll do it. They just want to see her face when she sees little Morey come sailing down."

Just then, Mrs. Yount walked in. "All right, students, let's find our seats," she said.

Just the idea of the poor little hamster being thrown out the window made Chelley too mad to think. Almost before she knew it, she turned to Mrs. Yount and raised her hand.

"Stop It"

The sudden silence in the room told Chelley that everyone was staring at her. With her face hot enough to glow in the dark, she tried to slide down out of sight. But Mrs. Yount had already seen her.

"Yes, Chelley?"

"Uh, I, uh." Chelley stared at the floor as she stammered. "I just wondered if we're going to be working on our science projects today."

"Yes, we are," Mrs. Yount answered. "Right after social studies. Now, if everyone will take out their social studies books, we'll get started."

When they did get together for science, Caitlin whispered, "For a second, I thought you were going to tell Mrs. Yount about Chris and Steven's plan."

Chelley shook her head. "I wanted to, but I got embarrassed. I just get really nervous when everyone is looking at me."

Shyness; making friends; being an example

"I'll say you do," Caitlin agreed. "You should see how red your face gets. See, you're getting red again. But don't worry. I always say I'm going to tell on those two myself, but I don't. I guess I'm afraid that everyone will be mad at me. Or that Chris and Steven will start playing tricks on me."

Chelley was amazed. "You're afraid everyone will be mad at you? But everyone likes you!"

"No," Caitlin said with a laugh, "everyone likes Andrea. If she gets mad at you, no one will be your friend."

"Why?" Chelley asked. "What makes her so special?"

Caitlin shrugged. "That's just the way the kids here think. Who knows why? I don't worry about it much. Whether I have friends here or not, I still have my horse. And my sister is going to teach me how to barrel-race."

Chelley smiled. "So, you have a quarter horse."

Caitlin looked surprised. "How did you know that?"

"I know that most people who do barrel racing at rodeos

use quarter horses," Chelley answered.

Caitlin was impressed. "You know a lot about horses for someone who lives in the city. Did you ever own one?"

"No. I'm just interested." Chelley's smile froze when Mrs. Yount stepped up.

"Girls, unless you're planning to drop horses out of the window, I suggest you get busy with your science project."

"Yes, ma'am," Caitlin said. Chelley just turned red. "I got an idea last night," Caitlin went on. "My sister said that a lot of people in her class wrapped their eggs in a big ball of cloth or paper. I saw an old flat basketball in our garage. What if we cut it open, stuff it full of soft paper or cloth, and put the egg in the middle?"

"Good idea," Chelley agreed. "If we tape it well, it won't pop open when it hits the ground. And the egg should be safe with that much padding. When can we put it together?"

Caitlin chewed on her pencil. "We really should practice it once to see if the egg breaks. Hey, why don't you come to my house after school? I'll get an egg from my mom, and we'll throw the basketball from the barn loft."

Chelley grinned. "I'll call my mother at lunchtime."

When she walked through the door that evening, Chelley was still grinning. "Mom! I'm home!"

Mom appeared with the phone stuck to her ear. "I'm talking to your father. He wants to know if you had a good time."

"Tell him Yes," Chelley answered. "Oh, and tell him thanks for helping me make a friend." As she walked to the refrigerator, Chelley heard her mother's voice.

"I don't know why she said that. Ask her when you get home."

Chelley grabbed two carrots and headed to the backyard.

"Hi, Benjamin," she said as she stuck one carrot through her rabbit's cage. One wiggle of his nose led to some serious chomping. With her own carrot between her teeth, Chelley opened the cage and brought her pet out to sit on her lap.

"I sure had fun today, Benjamin," she said as they both crunched another bite. "Our basketball egg didn't break, and we spent most of the afternoon playing around the barn and with Caitlin's horse."

Benjamin paused between bites. "Don't worry," Chelley added with a little squeeze. "I still like you better than any horse. But it sure is nice to have a friend to play with." As she stroked the rabbit's soft fur, she thought about Morey. "I'd never let anyone throw you out a window. Even if it meant not having any friends."

On the morning of the big egg drop, the classroom was buzzing louder than normal. Chelley tried not to notice Chris and Steven as they whispered and laughed and looked at the hamster cage. *I should tell Mrs. Yount. She would stop them,* Chelley thought. But she knew she wouldn't.

"I'll be waiting down below," Mrs. Yount said at science time. "One member of each team should come with me." Once she was on the ground, Mrs. Yount began to call names. "Andrea. You're first." Andrea tossed a big roll of paper towels out the window. The egg inside the tube didn't break. "Very good," Mrs. Yount called. "Chelley!"

As Chelley turned to pick up the basketball, she saw Chris reach into the hamster cage and pull Morey out. The parachute was in his other hand.

"Stop it!" Chelley shouted. Out loud. Chris froze. Chelley's face got red, but she said it anyway. "If you don't put him back, I'll tell Mrs. Yount right now."

"Aw, come on," Chris started to say. "It's not going to hurt you."

"But it might hurt Morey," Chelley said. "Play your stupid tricks some other way." From the window, they could hear Mrs. Yount calling for Chelley. Chelley just stared at Chris until he put the hamster back into the cage.

Then she leaned out the window and tossed the basketball toward Caitlin. It thudded on the ground, and Caitlin raced over to open it up. "It worked!" she shouted, holding up the unbroken egg. Chelley waved, then stepped back. Without

looking at the faces of the other kids, she went and sat at her desk.

By lunchtime, everyone had heard about what Chelley had done. "You really forced Chris to put the hamster back?" Caitlin asked. "You're braver than I am."

"No, I'm not," Chelley said. "I just couldn't let him hurt Morey." As she talked, Andrea walked up to their table.

"Hi! Can I sit with you guys?" she asked. Sitting beside Caitlin, she looked across at Chelley. "I'm glad you stopped Chris and Steven this morning. I didn't want them to do it either, but I didn't think I could stop them."

Chelley almost choked on her milk. "Thanks."

"And don't worry about them pulling tricks on you. We'll keep our eyes open. Right, Caitlin?"

"Right," Caitlin agreed. "Friends stick together." She held up her milk carton. So did Andrea. "Right, Chelley?"

Chelley's face got a little red, but she lifted her carton. "Right."

THE LAST STICK OF GUM

"Mom, can we get this?" Christina held up a T-shirt. "It'll go great with my jeans."

Her mother looked, then shook her head. "Christina, you have enough shirts. We can't afford to buy any more today."

Christina rolled her eyes and snapped her gum. "You always say that. Please? This is the only thing I'll get today. OK?"

"Christina, I'm sorry we're not rich enough to buy everything you want, but that's just the way it is. Our money only goes so far."

"We always have enough money for the things you want to buy," Christina added with a pout. She watched her mother's lips get tight and her eyes get narrow.

"Yes, I'm always wasting money on stuff like food and rent. I'm sorry you don't understand, but that's the way it is. So stop whining for everything you see."

What's her problem? Christina asked herself. *I just want the*

Dealing with unfairness; disappointment

kind of things everyone else has. It's not my fault we don't have enough money.

She didn't even ask her mother to buy more gum. She just bought a small pack with her own money.

The next morning, Christina plopped down next to Keisha on the bus. "Did you study for science?" Keisha asked, looking up from her book.

"Yeah," Christina answered, "for about an hour." She snapped her gum.

"Good. You can help me." Keisha handed her the book. "Ask me some questions. But first, give me some gum."

Christina handed over a stick, then asked, "What kind of electricity do you get when you rub your feet across a carpeted floor?"

"Static," Keisha answered. Forty questions and two more sticks of gum later, they arrived at school. As usual, Tara was waiting for them at the school door.

"Come on. We still have time to study," she said.

"We studied all the way here," Christina said. "Go ahead, ask me anything." By the time the first bell rang, the three girls felt like they were ready.

"Well?" Christina dropped her lunch tray onto the table. "How many did you get wrong?"

"I'm not sure about two," Tara said. "I know I got the rest right."

Keisha opened her milk carton. "Unless we studied wrong, I got them all right. What about you, Christina?"

"I might have missed three or four, but I'm happy." When the girls dumped their trash and returned their trays, she popped her last stick of gum into her mouth.

"Hey, give me some gum," Tara said, holding out her hand.

The Last Stick of Gum

Christina shrugged. "That was my last piece. Sorry."

"Oh, come on," Tara said. "You always have gum. All I want is one piece."

"I'm sorry," Christina repeated. "I'm all out."

Tara folded her arms. "You always have a stick for the people you really like. Don't you like me?"

Christina held out both hands. "I don't have any. It's gone. No matter who asks me, I'll say No. What's wrong with you?"

Tara just turned and stomped away.

Christina shook her head. "What is her problem? Does she really think I wouldn't give her gum if I had it, that I'm just trying to be mean? Why would I study with her and eat with her if I didn't like her?"

Keisha didn't have an answer.

"I felt bad enough not to have any gum to share. But then she made me mad." Christina felt kind of mad the rest of the day. Tara was absent the next day, but her first morning back, she was waiting at the school door again. "Hi," she said when Christina and Keisha walked up. "Uh, Christina, sorry about that gum stuff the other day. Still friends?"

"Still friends," Christina agreed with a smile.

That evening, she still felt good. "Mom, can we try this kind of pizza?" she asked as they shopped through the frozen-food section.

Mom looked at the pizza, then at the price. "No, this is too expensive. We can buy fixings and make pizza if you want, though."

Christina put it back. Then she saw the ice cream. "Mom, this is the kind that Keisha likes best. Can't we try it, just this once?" Christina watched as her mom glanced at the price, then shook her head.

"I'm sorry, dear, but we just can't—"

"I know. We can't afford it," Christina finished for her. "We can't afford anything good." She turned her back, folded her arms, and waited for the lecture.

Her mom started. "Christina, I'm . . . " Then she stopped and pushed the cart away. Christina followed after a few seconds, but neither one said another word until the groceries were packed in the back of the car.

When she got in, Mom didn't put the keys in the ignition. She turned to Christina. "Sweetheart, when you ask for things that I can't give you, I feel bad. Really, it hurts me not to be able to give you all the things you want. You're a beautiful person and deserve to have everything."

Christina had to smile about that.

"Do you really think I'm keeping food or clothes from you just to be mean?"

Suddenly, Christina's eyes got big. Something about this conversation seemed familiar.

"Then when you keep asking or you insist that I'm being mean, I get—"

"Mad," Christina finished for her. "You get mad. Of course. I did the same thing." She told her mom about Tara and the gum. "I got mad too. Could she really believe I wouldn't give it to her if I had it? But I didn't realize I was doing the same thing to you. I'm sorry, Mom."

Her mother's face lighted up with a big smile. "I'm just glad you understand. It's OK to want things, dear, and to ask for them. Just try to understand when I have to say No."

"I will, Mom." Christina smiled too. Then it turned into a frown. "But, Mom? I really need some more gum."

Mom laughed. "Gum we can afford. Come on. Let's go back and get it."

WHAT'S WRONG WITH YOUR MOM?

For this project, you'll be working in teams of two," Mrs. Novak announced. "Please select a partner, and begin working on your plans."

Cameron didn't have to think about whom he would work with. He turned his desk around. "Well, what kind of science project do you want to do this year?"

Courtney pushed her glasses back up on her nose. "The volcano we built last year was great. It's going to be hard to top that. You want to go by the library after school and look through the science section?"

Since Cameron and Courtney lived on the same street, they usually walked home together. In fact, even though the other kids teased them, they had been doing it since first grade.

"OK," Cameron agreed. "Let's look up something on weather. I'd like to figure out why it rains."

After school, Cameron waited in front of the school. "Hey,

Drinking in the family

Courtney," he called as she walked up, "did you see Alyssa anywhere?"

"The first grade was just getting out when I came by," Courtney answered. "She's coming." Sure enough, Cameron's little sister skipped up to them a few seconds later.

"Come on," Cameron said, "Courtney and I want to stop by the library for a few minutes."

"Cam, I'm supposed to bring cookies for our party tomorrow," Alyssa said as they started walking. "I told Mom, but she didn't make any."

Courtney answered before Cameron could say anything. "Ask her to make those great butterscotch cookies, Alyssa. Those were wonderful! Cam, you used to invite me over for those cookies all the time. Are you hogging them all for yourself now?"

Alyssa started to answer. "Mom doesn't make cookies anymore, since—"

Cameron interrupted. "Mom is too busy to make cookies very often. I'll share some with you next time, Courtney. Alyssa, don't forget. We can't check any books out. You can just look at them while we're here."

Courtney was shocked. "You can't check out any books? Why not?"

Cameron shrugged. "We had too many fines for bringing them back late. I kept losing my books." Then, before Courtney could ask any more questions, he started talking about their science project again. "Do you think we could make lightning? That would be better than a volcano."

Later, when they stopped in front of Courtney's house, she asked, "Do you want to work on math together tonight? I could come over after supper."

What's Wrong With Your Mom?

"No," Cameron said quickly. "I mean, sure, let's do our homework. I'll come to your house after my dad gets home."

Courtney started to ask another question, but didn't. She just smiled and said, "See you then."

At their own house, Cameron and Alyssa opened the door quietly. "Mom, are you home?" Alyssa called softly. There was no answer.

"Go ahead and watch TV for a while," Cameron said. "I'll peel us an apple." When he opened the refrigerator, there were some green things, but they weren't apples. There was green mold on a plate and some things that used to be vegetables.

I'd better clean those things out, Cameron decided. He was scraping gross things into the trash when Alyssa came in.

"Where's my apple?" she asked.

"We don't have any apples. How about a piece of bread with butter on it?" She left happy, and Cameron got back to work. By the time his dad got home, the refrigerator was mostly clean—and mostly empty.

"So, what's for supper, Cam?" Dad asked. "Is Mom home?"

Cameron shook his head. "We haven't seen her. Do you think she went to the grocery store? We need more food."

"If she doesn't go shopping, I'll go tomorrow. Have you done your homework?"

"Not yet." Cameron couldn't help sounding a little annoyed. "I've been in here cleaning since I got home. I'm going over to Courtney's after supper to do math."

"OK," Dad answered. "Thanks, buddy. I guess we all have to pitch in until Mom gets better."

Later, at Courtney's, the math homework was done quickly. "So," Courtney asked, "is your mom making those butterscotch cookies for Alyssa?"

Cameron smacked his forehead with his hand. "I forgot about that! I'd better go." He grabbed his books and papers while Courtney watched with a puzzled look on her face.

"Cam, what's going on? Is your mom sick or something?"

Cameron shook his head. "She's just been really busy. I'll see you later."

Since his mom still wasn't home, Cameron pulled out her recipe to see if he could make the cookies. "I guess we have everything," he said as he started to pour some flour into a bowl. "I hope this works."

When he pulled the cookies out of the oven, they smelled right. "Alyssa, come try a cookie," he called. Alyssa raced in to take a big bite.

"It thasths fuddy," she reported with her mouth full. "But ith good."

Cameron tried a bite. "You're right. They do taste different. I wonder what I did wrong. Oh, well. I'll put them in a bag for you in the morning."

Cameron was already in bed when he heard the door slam.

His mother was home. Before long, it started, just like he
knew it would.

"Where have you been? Out drinking again?" His dad's
voice was loud enough to be heard all over the house.

"I was just out with my friends." His mom's answer was
just as loud. "Shouldn't I be able to have a little fun once in a
while?"

"Once in a while! This is the third time this week!"

Cameron wrapped his pillow around his head. *I hate this,*
he thought for the thousandth time. *I hate it when she drinks
and when they fight.*

"Cam?" Alyssa's voice came quietly from the doorway.
"Can I sleep in your room?"

"Sure," he said. "Bring your pillow and blanket." Alyssa fell
asleep quickly, but Cameron was awake for a long time.

BUTTER-SCOTCH COOKIES

21

Hey," Courtney said in the cafeteria the next day, "your mom did make those cookies." She saw the ones Cameron had put in his lunch. "Can I have one?"

"Uh, I guess," Cameron stammered.

"His mom makes the best cookies," Courtney announced to the other kids around the table as she took a bite. "These butterscotch ones are my . . ." She stopped talking for a second. "Cam, these taste different than I remember."

Cameron grinned. "It's been so long since she made them, I guess she forgot how." He got busy eating his own cookie before she could ask any more questions. Courtney didn't say anything, but she stared at him for a long time.

For the next few weeks, Cameron and Courtney worked on their weather project. Cameron worked on the background poster that explained how clouds form, while Courtney planned a way to make a cloud inside their old aquarium.

"I think we can finish it tomorrow," Courtney said.

Drinking in the family

"I hope so, since the science fair is on Monday," Cameron replied. "Well, I have to be home in time for supper. I'll see you tomorrow."

For once, things seemed normal at his house. Cameron stood on the front porch and listened. Through the living-room window, he could hear his mother and sister talking and laughing. For some reason, the sound made him angry. He tried to slip by to his room without being noticed.

"Cameron, is that you?" He couldn't ignore his mother, so he joined them in the kitchen. "Alyssa and I were just going to make cookies. Do you want to help us?"

"No, thanks. I have homework to do."

Mom snapped her fingers. "That reminds me. Mrs. Cooper called and asked if I could bring cookies to the science fair for refreshments. I'd better call her back."

Cameron thought fast. "You're going to tell her you can't make it, right? That you have to work late or something?"

She picked up the phone. "What's wrong, Cameron? Don't you want me around? I'll be there to see your science project. I wouldn't miss that for anything."

Yes, you would, Cameron thought. *You'd miss it for another drink.* He listened while she told Mrs. Cooper that she would be happy to bring cookies. "As many as you need," she offered. Cameron just shook his head.

"See? It's going to be fun. Right, baby?" she asked Alyssa.

"Right!" Alyssa threw her arms around her mother's neck. Cameron couldn't take it anymore. He stalked into the living room.

Mom followed him in. "Cameron, what's wrong?"

Cameron stared at her for a second. "Why can't you be the same all the time? Sometimes, you're like this, and everything is great. But then you get drunk, and everything is terrible."

"Cameron! I might have a drink or two once in a while, but I'm not a drunk. I can quit anytime I want to."

"Good," Cameron said. "Then stop now. See how happy everyone is tonight? It can be like this all the time if you just stop drinking."

His mother smiled. "OK, I will. Starting now."

Then the doorbell rang. When Cameron opened it, Courtney was standing there. From the look on her face, Cameron knew she had heard everything through the window.

"I, uh, just wanted to ask about our math assignment," she said nervously.

"You mean you were just snooping around other people's business," Cameron said. "Why don't you just leave us alone!" Then he slammed the door.

Cameron had a hard time going to sleep that night. He didn't know if it was because Courtney knew about his mom's problem or because he didn't believe his mother's promise to stop drinking.

When Cameron saw Courtney the next Monday in front of the school, he did something he had never done before. He walked right past her without saying a word.

"Cam, wait a minute." He ignored her. "Cameron!" She shouted it loud enough for everyone to hear.

"OK." He stopped on the sidewalk. "You don't have to yell."

"I don't have to if you'll come here and talk to me." Courtney pushed her glasses back up on her nose. "What is wrong with you?"

Cameron walked back to her. "You heard that already on

my porch. You don't have to pretend to be my friend or anything."

Courtney's mouth fell open. "Are you talking about your
mother's problem?" Cameron could only nod. "Well, that's
exactly what it is—your mother's problem. Not yours."

"Courtney, you can't just pretend—"

Courtney stomped her foot. "I can do whatever I want! We
didn't stop being friends in second grade because everyone
was teasing us. We didn't stop being friends last year when
Eddie was telling those lies about me. So we're not going to
stop being friends because your mother has a problem!"

Suddenly, Cameron couldn't keep from smiling. "OK."

Courtney was all business. "Now, I looked up some things
in the library this weekend. Your mother is an alcoholic. That
means she can't control how much she drinks, and she can't
stop drinking on her own."

"Yes, she can. You heard her say she would. She hasn't been drunk since then."

Courtney just looked at him. "Cam, how many times has she said that before?" He didn't answer. "She doesn't think she even has a problem."

Cameron didn't have an answer. Courtney went on. "I talked to Mrs. Novak yesterday."

"You told our science teacher? About my mom? Courtney!"

Courtney stomped her foot again. "No, I didn't tell her. Remember, last year when my grandfather died, and I was sad? Mrs. Novak really helped me. So I called her yesterday and asked her what a kid should do if one of her parents was an alcoholic."

Cameron was interested. He forgot to be mad. "What did she say?"

"She told me that there's a group that meets every week to support kids and families who are dealing with an alcoholic. She said it helps them a lot. And I believe her."

While Cameron shook his head slowly, the bell rang. "Let's go before we're late to class," he said. He knew Courtney was trying to help. But inside, he was thinking, *Maybe this time, Mom really will stop.*

THE HARDEST THING

T he closer it was to the science fair that evening, the more nervous Cameron got. It wasn't about his project. He knew that was fine. "Dad, is Mom really going tonight?" he asked.

"Sure, son. We both want to see you win another blue ribbon." But when Mom wasn't home when it was time to leave, Cameron didn't feel too bad. "I'm sure Mom will be along soon," Dad said as they parked by the school.

I hope not, Cameron thought. But before the judging even began, he heard her voice.

"Well, here's where you all went," she said loudly. Too loudly. Several people turned to stare at her.

"Oh no," Cameron moaned. "Look at her hair."

"And her makeup," Courtney added. "She looks like Halloween."

Cameron heard another parent talking. "What's wrong with that woman?" she asked. "Is she drunk or something?"

Drinking in the family

The Hardest Thing

"We
have to get
her out of here," Courtney decided. "Come on."

But Mrs. Cooper got to her first. "Oh, there you are," she gushed. "Did you take the cookies to the kitchen already?"

Cameron's mom looked at her curiously. "Did I do what?" she asked, weaving slightly.

"The cookies," Mrs. Cooper said again. "You said you

The Hardest Thing

would bring eight dozen butterscotch cookies for our program this evening. You didn't forget, did you?"

Cameron rushed up and grabbed his mother's arm. "Of course not. Let's go out and get them." He tried to lead her back toward the door.

"Wait," Mrs. Cooper said, "I'll get someone to help carry them."

"I'll help," Courtney said quickly. "We'll be fine." When they got her to the car, Cameron rushed back in to find his dad. The trip home was quiet. Too quiet. Dad let them both off at the curb.

"I have to go back and get your sister," he told Cameron. "Try to get your mother into bed."

Cameron tried, but his mom stopped at the laundry room. "I just have to get something," she said. Cameron knew what it was. She hid a new bottle behind the ironing board every week.

He went into the kitchen to look for something to eat. By the time she staggered in, he was in the middle of fixing a sandwich. He looked up and tried to smile when she stepped into the kitchen. "Hi, Mom. I'm just making a sandwich so you won't have to worry about supper."

Her red eyes and wild hair were scary enough. But her voice gave Cameron shivers. "Are you sayin' I can't fix supper? You think you're too good for my cookin'?"

"I'm just trying to help, Mom." Cameron picked up his sandwich and edged around her. "Why don't you go lie down for a while?"

"You'll stay here until you eat my supper!" Mom shouted. She lurched toward the stove and grabbed at the frying pan.

"Mom, stop!" Cameron pulled her back. "You're just going

to hurt yourself." She whirled around and grabbed him by the shoulders.

With her face two inches from his, she shouted, "You think I'm too drunk to cook? I'll have you know I'm still the mother in this house!"

Something inside Cameron snapped. "No, you're not! You stopped being the mother when you started drinking! I hate you when you're drunk!"

Her hand slapped him right across the face.

It hurt worse than anything Cameron had ever felt. But he just stood there and stared back into her eyes. "I still hate you," he repeated. Then he jerked away and ran out the front door.

He was still on the porch when Alyssa and his dad drove up. "Alyssa, go on to your room," Dad said. "I'll be there in a minute." To Cameron, he said, "Sorry about missing your science fair. I guess your mom just wasn't up to it tonight."

Cameron was still mad. "Come on, Dad. She wasn't up to it? She was drunk. Again. And it's driving me crazy!" He rushed on before his dad could speak. "We need to get some help. Mom needs to go to a hospital for alcoholics."

His dad was quiet for a long time. Finally, he said, "Cameron, I really don't think we can do that. It might just make it worse, not better."

"I don't see how it could get any worse," Cameron mumbled, rubbing his cheek.

The next morning, he met Courtney in front of the school. "Sorry about having to leave last night," he told her.

"That's OK," she answered. "We won third place. How is your mom?"

"Worse," Cameron admitted. "She hit me last night. And Dad still isn't sure what to do."

Courtney got mad. "What is he waiting for? For her to really hurt you? Or for her to hurt Alyssa?"

That made up Cameron's mind. "Courtney, will you go talk to Mrs. Novak with me? We might be late to math."

Courtney shrugged and smiled. "I didn't do my homework anyway."

When Mrs. Novak's door closed behind them, Cameron took a deep breath. It was the hardest thing he had ever done,

but he said it. "Mrs. Novak, I think my mother is an alcoholic."

Deep inside, Cameron began to hope that things really were going to get better.

PAJAMA ROLLER SKATING

Lucy, are you on that phone again?"

Lucy frowned toward the sound of her mother's voice. "Mom, I'm calling Megan." After she pushed the right buttons, Lucy waited. "Megan? No, I still haven't asked. Yes, I want to come to your slumber party. But I might have to do something with my mom or dad."

Megan laughed. "You have the busiest schedule of any kid I know."

"You're lucky," Lucy replied. "Your parents are together. Since mine got divorced, I have to keep up with two different schedules. I mean, I'm glad they both want to do things with me. But sometimes I forget *who* I'm supposed to be with *when*. And they both look lonely a lot. So I have to do things with them to keep them happy."

Suddenly, a red light on the phone started flashing. "Megan, there's a call on the other line. I have to put you on hold." Then she hit another button. "Hello? Oh yes, she's

> ### Asking for what you need;
> ### living with divorced parents

here. Just a minute, please." She clicked back to Megan's line. "It's a call for my mother. I have to go."

"See you later," Megan said. "And don't forget the party."

That evening, Lucy tried to find a way to ask. "What are you doing tomorrow night, Mom?" she asked.

"I want to take you shopping at that new store in the mall," her mother answered. "And the Clothes Closet is having a sale."

Before Lucy could answer, the phone rang. "I'll get it," she said quickly, running into the living room. "Hello? Oh, hi, Megan." The phone cord twisted around her finger. "No, I haven't. I'm trying! It's not as easy as you think." While she talked, the red light flashed again. "Megan, someone else is calling. Just a second."

Lucy pushed the button. "Hello? Hi, Dad."

Pajama Roller Skating

"Lucy, you have to come over tomorrow night. The Badgers are playing a double-header. We can make popcorn and watch the whole thing right here."

Lucy almost dropped the phone. "Uh, Dad, I—"

He interrupted. "It was so great to have you over last week. It felt like the good old days. I know it's almost bedtime, so I'll stop talking. But I'll pick you up around seven tomorrow! 'Bye."

"But, Dad—Dad!" Lucy stared at the phone. "Oh no." For a second, she forgot about Megan. Then she stabbed the button. "Megan, I—"

"Lucy, I have to get off the phone now," Megan said without waiting. "I'll see you tomorrow about seven. 'Bye."

"Megan, wait!" But all she heard was the buzz of the dial tone. Before she could even set the phone down, her mother walked in.

"Lucy, it's time for bed. You'll have to talk to Megan tomorrow."

"But, Mom!"

Her mother held up one hand. "Don't start. You need your rest tonight if we're going to stay out late shopping tomorrow." She smiled. "It's going to be great! Good night, Lucy." Then she walked away.

For a few seconds, Lucy just sat there, frozen in place. Finally, she let the phone fall to the table and staggered toward her room. "What am I going to do now?" she moaned to herself. Going through the motions without thinking about them, Lucy almost brushed her teeth with shampoo.

With the toothpaste on her toothbrush, she stared in the mirror while she brushed. *Dad's lonely. I'm the only person he has to do things with. So I should watch the game with him. But*

Mom doesn't have many friends either. So I should go and be with her. After she rinsed and spit, Lucy stared at herself again.

"But if I don't go to Megan's slumber party, she's going to think I don't like her," Lucy said out loud. "How am I going to keep everyone happy?"

Even after her head fell onto the pillow, her thoughts were still spinning around. *I'll never get to sleep,* Lucy thought. But before she knew it, she was asleep—and dreaming.

Swish, swish. Lucy was skating down the middle of the mall. "The new store is this way," her mother said as she skated along beside Lucy, carrying a plastic shopping bag. She grabbed Lucy's right arm. "I know you want to go shopping."

Her dad was skating on the other side, with two bags of popcorn in his arms. "The TV store is showing the Badger game on their super-big screen." He grabbed Lucy's left arm. "I know you want to watch it. Let's go."

Before Lucy was pulled in two, Megan appeared right in front of her, wearing her pajamas and skates too. "Come on," she said. "The slumber party is starting." Megan grabbed Lucy's other arm and pulled that way. "I know that's what you want to do."

Looking around, Lucy realized that she was wearing her pajamas too—right in the middle of the mall. That bothered her more than having three arms. She yanked away from all three of them.

"How can any of you know what I want to do?" she shouted, "when I haven't told you!" Lucy skated away as fast as she could. "It's my life! I have to do some things for me!"

Lucy had to swerve around people who were laughing and pointing. Instead of getting away, she kept going slower and

Pajama Roller Skating

slower until it seemed like she was trying to skate through a thick cloud. She tried one last push—and fell out of bed onto the floor.

"Oh," Lucy moaned as she crawled back up. "Now I'm dreaming about it too." But as she remembered her dream, she realized what she had to do.

At breakfast, Lucy swallowed the last of her milk and took a deep breath. She waited until her mom was washing the dishes. Then she said, "Mom, can we go shopping another time? Megan's having a slumber party tonight, and she invited me to sleep over."

Her mother stopped and held a plate for a long second. "Sure we can, Lucy. Why didn't you tell me sooner?"

"I was afraid to," Lucy admitted. "I know you like to do things with me—and I didn't want you to be lonely."

"Lucy, I do like being with you," Mom said as she dried her hands on a towel. "But you need to do things with your friends. Promise me that you won't worry about me like that. I'm taking care of you, not the other way around."

Pajama Roller Skating

"OK," Lucy answered. "I promise. Thanks, Mom." A hug made it even better. Lucy felt brave enough to call her father.

"Dad?"

Her dad sounded happy. "Are you already ready for some baseball?"

Lucy swallowed hard. "Dad, can we watch baseball another night? Megan's having a slumber party tonight, and I want to go."

"A slumber party, huh?" To Lucy's surprise, her dad's voice still sounded happy. "That sounds like fun, honey. There'll be another game next week."

"You'll be OK?" Lucy asked. "I don't want you to be lonely."

"Hey, I'm the parent here," her dad answered. "I'm supposed to worry about you. I'll be fine. You have fun tonight."

Suddenly, Lucy felt good enough to skate through the mall backward—but not in her pajamas!

Window-Washing Spies

"Up and at 'em!" Dad called from the bottom of the stairs. "We don't want to be late!"

Zachary opened one eye. "We want to be asleep," he mumbled. Then he sat up and threw his pillow at the pile of covers in the other bed.

"Hey, leave me out of this," Travis grumbled. "I'm not getting up early just to work all day for no pay."

"Oh yes you are," Zachary said as he headed to the bathroom. "And if you lie there much longer, I'll eat all the eggs before you get to the kitchen."

"No, you won't," Travis announced, jumping out from under the covers and dashing toward the bathroom door. That started a race that ended with both boys leaping into their chairs at the kitchen table. "I won!" Travis called.

"No, I did," Zachary stated.

"I'm glad to see so much enthusiasm so early in the morning," Dad said with a smile. "If we put that behind a lawn

Being kind; what it means to be a Christian

mower or a scrub brush at the church, we'll be done in no time."

Suddenly, Travis and Zachary felt very tired. "Why do we have to work today?" Travis complained.

"It's our church," Mom answered. "Besides, you're not working for nothing. There'll be a big potluck lunch when we're finished. And I know how much both of you like those."

While they were stopped at a red light on the way to the church, Zachary nudged his brother. "Look!" he hissed, pointing at the parking lot to the right.

"Will work for food," Travis read from the sign a man was holding up. The man was sitting on the hood of an old station wagon. Inside was a woman and two little kids. "Hey, Dad," Travis said, "what does that mean—'will work for food'?"

Dad glanced at the sign. "Well, it means that man is very poor and will work anywhere today so he can eat."

"You mean so *they* can eat," Travis corrected him. "There's a family in the car. Shouldn't someone help them? We have lots of food."

The light changed, and Dad drove on. "It's not that simple. Some people use signs like that to get people to stop, then all they want is money for drugs or alcohol."

"But what if those people are really hungry?" Travis asked.

Mom spoke up. "There are places in our town that serve free meals to anyone who comes in. And there are shelters that homeless people can live in. Our church gives money to both of those, so we are helping."

Zachary was staring out the back window. "We could offer to let them go work with us today," he said. "After all, isn't that what we're doing? Working for food?"

Dad looked over at Mom. "We could invite them," Mom

said. At the next corner, they turned around. Dad rolled down his window as they drove up next to the old station wagon.

"Good morning," he called to the man. "If you're interested, we're headed to our church for some general clean-up work— mowing, dusting, cleaning. We'll be sharing a big picnic meal at lunchtime. You're welcome to join us."

The man turned and spoke to his wife in the car. Then he stood up, nodding. "That would be great."

"Then just follow us," Dad said with a smile. At the church, Travis and Zachary watched while their dad introduced the man to Pastor Evans. "Pastor, this is Tim Endicott and his family. They were looking for work today, and we were looking for workers."

While they were standing there, Travis and Zachary heard some other church members talking quietly to each other. "I know a guy who picked up one of those will-work-for-food guys. The guy only worked a few hours. Then he disappeared.

But the next day, my friend's place was robbed. He thinks the homeless guy did it."

"Did you hear that?" Zachary whispered. "What if they're really here to steal?"

Travis frowned. "We'd better keep an eye on them, Zach. We talked Dad into stopping and asking them. If they steal from the church, it'll be our fault."

They watched as Pastor Evans handed the man a pair of hedge trimmers. "Why don't you work on the bushes along this side of the church. I'll send someone around with a wagon to collect the branches."

Then they heard their dad's voice. "Boys, I've got just the job for you. Here are the hose, a bucket of soapy water, a sponge, and a squeegee. Wash the outside of all the church windows."

Before long, Travis was washing the windows with the sponge while Zachary rinsed with the hose and then wiped the window off. "How are we going to keep an eye on the Endicotts from here?" Travis asked. "Mr. Endicott's on the other side of the church."

"I have to go to the bathroom anyway," Zachary said. "I'll check on him when I go by." He dropped the hose and snuck around the corner. In just a few minutes, he was back.

"Well?" Travis asked.

Zachary flopped down to the ground. "It's just what we thought. I saw him put Pastor Evans's pocketknife in his pocket. You know, that big brown knife the pastor used at the campfire last summer?"

Travis's shoulders slumped. "Just what we were afraid of. I wonder how he got his hands on it so fast? And what do we do now?"

"I don't know," Zachary said. He stood up and grabbed the hose as they moved down to the next window. As Travis washed it off with the sponge, Zachary added, "I still don't think they are thieves. They seem like nice people."

"Shh!" Travis hissed. He stared through the glass into the church kitchen. "Look at this."

Zachary stared in too. "So?"

"That's Mrs. Endicott. Why is she going through all the cupboards and the pantry?" Travis turned away. "And why is she writing in that notebook?"

Zachary caught on. "She could be making a list of things to steal."

"Or writing down a plan to break back into the church later, like tonight when everyone's gone." Travis collapsed to the ground. "So what are we going to do?"

"Wait a Minute!"

There's only one thing to do," Zachary announced. Then he hit his brother with a spray from the hose.

"Hey, cut that out!" Travis shouted, waving his arms to block the water. Then he changed his mind. "Do it again. That felt good."

Before long, they were both soaking wet. By the time he looked in the window again, Mrs. Endicott was gone. As they washed the next window, Zachary said, "Travis, I wish we hadn't stopped and talked to the Endicotts. But I kept thinking, what if they really were hungry?"

"I know," Travis agreed. "We get hungry before lunch every day, but we know there's food in the kitchen. It's not fair that some people don't even have food."

"Or a kitchen," Zachary added. "I thought that's what Christians are supposed to do—take care of people who were in need." With another squirt of water, he made up his mind. "I'm not telling anyone anything until after we eat. Even if

Being kind; what it means to be a Christian

they're the kind of people who are trying to steal, at least they'll get something good to eat today."

Before long, Dad showed up. "Hey, it's getting close to lunchtime," he said. "But I guess it would be impossible for you guys to finish all these windows before we eat."

Travis looked at Zachary. "Impossible? I don't think so. Come on, Zach." For a few minutes, the boys forgot about stealing and spying. But they got all the windows clean in time to line up at the picnic tables.

"Friends, before we eat," Pastor Evans said, "I'd like to thank you all for your help. It's nice to belong to a family that cares about their house and about each other. I'd especially like to thank our new friends, Tim and Louise Endicott and their family. They've been a big help this morning."

After the blessing, Zachary was glad to see the pastor invite the Endicotts to go first in line. *Now I know they'll get something good to eat, even if the police come and arrest them later.*

"When do we tell?" Travis whispered as he finished off his dessert.

"Is Dad finished yet?" Zachary asked. "Let's tell him—he'll know what to do."

"There's Dad," Travis said, "talking to Pastor Evans. Let's go tell them both." But as they reached that table, Pastor Evans stood up.

"Friends, before you all begin leaving, I wanted to share something else with you. I've learned that it was two of our younger members who insisted that we expand our church family today and invite the Endicotts."

Zachary and Travis froze. *No, don't tell them that!* Zachary thought. But by the look on the pastor's face and their father's proud look, he knew what was coming next. Travis looked like his dessert wasn't going to stay in his stomach.

"Zachary and Travis are good examples to all of us today," Pastor Evans said. "Christians should always be looking for someone who needs a helping hand. Thanks, boys, for setting a good example for us all today."

Before Zachary could say anything, the Endicotts joined them. "Thank you very much," Mrs. Endicott said. "This is the best meal our children have had all week." The tears in her eyes made Zachary's face turn red.

Mr. Endicott shook both of their hands. "We moved to this town last month because I was offered a good job," he told everyone. "But when we got here, the company didn't hire me after all. Now we've run out of money completely. I guess I'd better get back out there and keep looking for a job. So we'd better get going."

Travis elbowed his brother. "What are we going to do?" he mouthed. Zachary shrugged, then grabbed the pastor's arm.

"Wait a minute, Pastor Evans," he tried to whisper. "There's something we need to . . ."

Pastor Evans interrupted. "Just a moment, Zachary. Tim, don't leave so quickly. Anyone who will come and work like you two have today is serious about making a living. I'm sure we can make some calls and help you find a place to stay tonight. And tomorrow, I have a few ideas about jobs."

Travis tugged on the pastor's other sleeve. "Pastor Evans, you need to know . . ." But no one was listening.

Mr. Endicott seemed overwhelmed. "Thanks. More than I can say." He stuck his hands in his pockets and turned away. Suddenly, he turned back. "Oh, here's your knife," he said to Pastor Evans. "I forgot I had it. You were right. It cut the big branches faster."

Zachary stopped breathing. Travis's eyes almost popped out. Before either one could move, Mrs. Endicott spoke up. "And here's that list of things in the church kitchen," she said to their mom. "I marked the ones that you're all out of."

"Thanks so much," Mom said. "Now we'll know what to shop for. Why don't we go back in and see if there's anything you can use for supper tonight."

People began walking away, but Zachary sat down on the picnic bench and wiped his forehead. "Boy, was that close," he said to Travis.

Travis agreed. "Let's not tell anyone what we were thinking. Let's just forget it."

But someone else hadn't forgotten. "Now, what was it that you wanted to tell me?" Pastor Evans asked.

"Uh, never mind," Zachary stammered. "See you later!" He grabbed Travis, and they ran.

Later, at home, Mom said, "I'm really proud of you two.

You did a good thing this morning when you talked us into stopping."

Zachary cleared his throat. "Well, the truth is, we thought the Endicotts might be trying to steal from the church. We were spying on them," he admitted.

Dad laughed. "I was worried about that too. I guess I tried to keep an eye on them also, because some people don't turn out to be as nice as they did. I'm just glad we could help people who really needed our help."

"I just didn't like the idea of them being hungry," Travis said. "In fact, I'm getting hungry just thinking about it. Mom, when's supper?"

ATTACK OF THE BOOKS

eter, what are you watching?"

Peter stabbed at the buttons on the remote, but he was too slow. His dad saw the machine guns blasting away before the TV clicked off.

"Peter?"

"Dad, it's just Spencer Spy. And there's this monster thing—anyway, it's a good show."

"And the machine gun is just there for decoration?"

Peter squirmed. "Not exactly. But he doesn't shoot anyone unless he has to. He's really a good guy."

Dad sat on the couch by Peter. "Son, maybe he is the good guy in this story. The problem is that you're not old enough to watch this kind of show."

"But, Dad! It's not a bad show."

"Then why did you turn it off when I came in? We have rules about what kind of shows you can watch. If I can't trust you to live by those rules when I'm not looking, then I can't

Television; making good choices

let you watch TV when I'm not with you."

Peter ended up being sent to his room.

He flopped back onto his pillow. *I'm old enough to decide what's good to watch. Am I supposed to watch little-kid shows? Or read books all the time?* He grabbed his reading book off the desk beside his bed. "I hate books!" he said out loud. Then, just to show how mad he was, he threw it at the bookshelf by the wall.

Smack! It hit the top shelf. That shelf came loose and tipped. Almost in slow motion, the books began to slide. "Oh no," Peter moaned. He dashed over to try to stop them. But when they fell, they tipped the next shelf and the next. Peter could only duck.

Thunk, thunk, thunk. Finally, books stopped falling, and Peter staggered back to his bed. "Ow," he said, rubbing his head. He closed his eyes. "Attacked by books—it figures."

Rubbing his head, Peter just lay there, thinking. His eyes stayed closed, and he drifted off to . . .

"Psst!"

Peter's eyes popped open.

"Hey, kid. Yeah, you. Over here, on the page."

Peter glanced around the room. Then his eyes settled on a book that was lying open on his desk.

"No, don't look at me!" the book said. "Pretend you don't see me."

Peter blinked. "I must have hit my head harder than I thought."

The book whispered, "We have a mission for you—a secret mission, full of danger. Can we count on you?"

Peter's mouth opened. "Wuh-I-duh . . ."

The pages of the book trembled. "What's that? Someone's

coming? Quick, chew this page up and swallow it! No, wait. Close the book, and then act casual. And don't forget what page we were on!"

Peter reached over and slammed the book closed, then lay back down and closed his eyes. He heard footsteps go by his door. After a few seconds, he opened his eyes and sat up.

"I must be losing my mind," he said. "I know I wasn't just talking to a book." To prove it, he reached over and opened the book again.

"All clear now?" the book said. "Good. OK, come close—we'll have to whisper. I was sent to contact you with this message: There may be an enemy in this house! A one-eyed monster!"

"What?" Peter still didn't believe in the book, much less a monster.

The book continued. "We heard it from our cousins, the

magazines. They say it turns on its evil eye, and people do whatever it says. You haven't seen it, have you?"

"No," Peter said, very honestly. He had never seen a monster of any kind in his house.

The book nodded. "Don't be frightened. The books have everything under control. We attack tonight!"

"How?" Peter asked.

The book was offended. "What do you mean, how? We'll march right down there and do battle. Oh, you think we can't march! This house has books of marching music, encyclopedias that explain marching—why, I myself have the word on pages forty-seven and one twenty-eight!"

Peter's eyes got big. "I never would have imagined."

"Here's the plan," the book said. "We need you to sneak into the living room and spy for us. Keep your eyes open for a large, one-eyed, square-shaped monster. When you have it located, retreat at once. We don't want you in any danger."

"A large, one-eyed, square-shaped monster," Peter repeated.

"Right. Then report back to me. I shall personally lead the books into battle!"

"You?" Peter said. "What kind of fighters are books?"

"Have you ever been hit by a shelf of books?"

Peter's hand went up to the bump on his head.

"Go now! Oh, but close me first. I don't want my pages to curl."

Peter was still rubbing his bump as he snuck out into the hall. "This is too weird," he mumbled. But it got worse. The hallway was too long for his house. And the living room was way too big. Peter was so amazed he almost forgot to spy.

"I don't see any monster in here," he said after a quick look around. "That book must be crazy. Or else I am."

"Don't be too sure," a voice said.

"What?" Peter jumped back. Then the television turned itself on. Its light gleamed like a big eye. "Hey, you're the monster! Stay back."

"Oh, please," the TV said. "I already have you captured."

"Not me," Peter said, backing up.

Somehow the TV pulled out a machine gun. "Oh, really. You'll watch anything that comes on, won't you? No matter if it's violent and hateful or just stupid and mean. You'll watch it, all right. You'll watch whatever I tell you to!" Then the TV raised the gun and started firing.

"No! Help!" Peter shouted, falling backward. Suddenly, out of nowhere, books started falling from the sky. Some stopped the bullets. Others piled on top of the TV.

"You did it, Peter," the book said. "We got the monster! Peter?"

"Peter?"

Peter's eyes snapped open. "Dad! It's you! I thought—" Peter sat up quickly. "I thought the books . . . I guess it was a dream."

"Well, supper's ready. Come on." As they walked through the living room, Peter kept one eye on the television. He still remembered what it said in the dream. "You'll watch whatever I tell you to!"

"Peter," Dad called from the kitchen, "when we finish eating, let's sit down and watch something good on TV."

"I don't know," Peter called back. "I'm thinking I might read a book."

Index

Each story in the *Great Stories for Kids* set has been carefully designed to teach one or more specific character-building lessons or spiritual values. This index will help you quickly find the lesson being taught in each story. Following the title of the story, the reference is given for the book and the page number in the set. For example, the first reference, **4**:143 indicates page 143 in Book 4 of the set.